THE VENETIAN GLASS NEPHEW

THE VENETIAN GLASS NEPHEW

by

ELINOR WYLIE

Published in 1984 by
Academy Chicago, Publishers
425 N. Michigan Ave.
Chicago, IL 60611

Published by arrangement with Alfred A. Knopf, Inc.

Printed and bound in the USA

Library of Congress Cataloging in Publication Data

Wylie, Elinor Hoyt, 1885–1928.
The Venetian glass nephew.

Reprint. Originally published: New York: G.H. Doran Co., 1925.

I. Title.
PS3545.Y45V4 1984 813'.52 84-14557
ISBN 0-89733-112-5 (pbk.)

TO WILLIAM, WITH MY LOVE

CONTENTS

Book One: PETER INNOCENT

"And then he wept a little, and fell
to talking of magic and macaroni."
—Prince de Ligne.

BOOK ONE: PETER INNOCENT

I: Blue Balloon

PETER INNOCENT BON was about to return to the Republic of Venice; although he had that very day entered upon the eighty-first year of his age, his eyes, blue as veronica flowers, were even now full of a child's tears. His heart was lighter than a flower; indeed, it danced so high and airily, and teased the tenuous cord of his mortality with such persistent malice, that he conceived of it as a toy balloon, an azure plaything in a pantomime, caught by a thread of gold to stable earth, and germane to the sky.

It will be unnecessary to explain to minds versed in such matters that Peter Innocent Bon must by no means be confounded with John Bona of Mondovi, a misapprehension imaginable in the ignorant, since both were cardinals and both distinguished scholars. But wider far than the mere century of time separating the lives of these holy men is the gulph that sunders their natures and their activities. Consanguinity there may have been, in reason, but the two were never spiritually akin. Peter Innocent undoubtedly possessed the Antwerp edition of his cousin's works, published in 1777, and the devotional treatise "De Sacrificio Missæ" was often in his hands; a few marginal notes attest to application saddened by bewilderment. To those desiring to achieve a better comprehension of the character of Peter Innocent Bon, cardinal priest and cardinal prefect of the Congregation of the Propaganda, the historian recommends a careful study of his poetical writings (Venice, 1790) and his notes upon liturgical subjects (Parma, 1794). His memoirs, surveying as they did almost the entire length of the eighteenth century with a bland and illuminative eye, must have contained matter of the highest interest; this valuable document was unfortunately destroyed by Madame de Staël in a passing fit of temper during the composition of "Corinne," merely because it contained a simple unadorned account of the coronation of Corilla Olimpica.

On this eighth of May, 1782, Peter Innocent, clad in the grey-brown garb of the Franciscan Friars Minor, stood dreaming among delicate grotesques in the porch of his titulary church of St. Bonaventura. It was evening; the Roman sun had lost its imperial savagery, and tempered light lay tenderly upon the cardinal's brow. His face, that had beheld the secular world for eighty years, was lifted to the more transparent heaven; forgetting Rome and even the Vatican, he regarded the Holy City above the horns of the new moon. He looked affectionately yet familiarly into the little loopholes of the stars, with none of the bitter hunger of the returning exile; to Peter Innocent the bread of earth was never salty, nor the stairs of heaven too steep. As a boy may see at evening the lighted windows of his mother's kitchen, he saw without surprise celestial preparation for his home-coming through a bright chink that may have been Aldebaran. Tugging at its gilded thread, his heart danced over him, a blue balloon in deeper aërial blue.

Above the chiselled silver of his head, his heart danced, expanded by happiness and an exquisite gratitude towards all humanity and the Son of God made man. In particular, his heart blessed the new pope, Pius VI, for although Giovanni Angelo Braschi had ruled Christendom for some seven years, Peter Innocent never thought of him save as a handsome innovation, superseding with the suavest courtesy the cardinal's dead patron and beloved friend, the Franciscan Clement XIV. Now this same Pius, whom Peter Innocent a little feared, the more that he was beautiful and brilliant and vain, proposed for reasons of his own to visit the green lagoons and golden palaces of Venice, having among his suite, again for reasons of his own, Peter Innocent Bon, cardinal prefect of the Congregation of the Propaganda.

The cardinal did not concern himself with reasons; he thought of Venice, and the bright thread pulled hard upon his heart. He had not seen that city for nearly thirty years; not since his brother Nicholas Bon was banished to the monastery of Venda by the Council of Ten and the Inquisitors of the Holy Office. In that same year Paul Dona was confined in the fortress of Palma, and five years later the noble Angelo Querini was imprisoned in the castle of St. Felice at Verona.

For a time the spirit of Peter Innocent suffered a faint infusion of bitterness throughout its milk and honey; he began to believe in spies and politics, and found himself disliking the Dominicans without feeling any particular love for the Jesuits. But he managed with admirable tact to hold himself aloof from all dissension, and it is certain that his veined patrician hand was not among those which upheld the fainting resolution of Lorenzo Ganganelli as the pontiff traced the momentous syllables of the brief, *Dominus ac redemptor* and signed it Clement, servant of the servants of God.

But this was years, and happy years, ago, and to-day Peter Innocent could remember that all these brave and liberal senators had been set free either by death or by the reforms of '63, and that Querini had travelled in Switzerland and become a valued friend of Voltaire's. The cardinal had long ago forgiven Venice, and upon this Ascension Eve his heart was a blue balloon because it was going home.

He thought of himself as a child upon other Ascension eves and morrows, in a past not dim at all, but radiant as a double dawn in sky and water. He saw the *Bucintoro* setting forth from Santa Lucia, a gilded barge arrayed in cloth of gold, with winged lions, tritons, nereids, painted with gold and burnished by the sun, with the great standard of the republic crackling like lightning overhead. He thought of the ancient glory of Venice, and of the Lion of the Evangelist. His grey habit of the Seraphic Order fell from his shoulders, and he was a child again, in a coat of sapphire velvet, with a silver feather in his cap.

Softly, very softly, the supple folds of dun-colour descended once more over this remembered magnificence, and Peter Innocent felt the worn, warm fabric about his fragile bones. Here, too, was cause for gratitude, for the new pope had permitted him to continue in this ingenuous disguise, first granted him by the generosity of Clement, so that he alone of the pontifical family went comfortably impoverished, clad in the mystic tatters of Assisi. Within a remote wing of the Vatican a wardrobe of ebony and figured brass guarded vestments of white and red and green, of violet and black and the more curious sheen of metal, with robes and rochets of a less sacral character and rich liturgical gloves and stockings, intermixed with honorific decorations.

Peter Innocent loved best to drift, elusive as a skeleton leaf, along the streets of Rome, recognized by all, but accosted by none save an occasional German traveller or English milord; the legerity of the French mind made the Gallic visitor quick to comprehend his desire for solitude, and the very transparency of the masking rendered it invulnerable. Whether or not he believed himself effectively disguised remained a mystery to the last. He spoke but little; indeed it was a common saying at the time that Clement had forgotten to unseal his mouth; his smile, however, impressed even the most impious as a small flame burning perpetually within the silver shadow of his countenance.

At the conclusion of Vespers, he often knelt in a sculptured recess of the Church of St. Bonaventura, while the words *O salutaris hostia* were borne upon the wings of ancient music towards the benediction. As the priest, his shoulders wrapped in the humeral veil, lifted the monstrance from the lighted altar and with it described in that already consecrated air the sign of the cross, the tears of Peter Innocent aspersed like holy water whatever evil might survive within those walls, beneath that vaulted nave.

II: Consider the Lilies

Near St. George in Alga, upon an iridescent morning of mid-May, the Doge and Signory of Venice received the pontiff and his suite, conveying them thence to the monastery of St. John and St. Paul, where they were sumptuously lodged. As the lacquered barge imposed its fan of ripples, like a peacock's tail, upon lagoon and narrowing canal, the visitors vied with one another in expressions of awe and contentment; they moved in the heart of a pearl whose orient skin was outer space. Peter Innocent alone was silent; his youth overwhelmed him as though every immemorial wave of the Adriatic were poured upon his pensive head. He bowed his face upon his folded hands; when he lifted his eyes again, they were dazzled by the great palaces of the Venetian patriciate, all arabesqued in marble and embossed by emblems. Here burned the silver torch of the Morosini; the silver ladder of the Gradenigo scaled the heavens; the five-leaved roses of the house of Loredan endured in frosted stone so delicate that it appeared to spread a perfume on the air.

The gondolas were black, but all their canopies were coloured like the parterres of a prince's garden. The sunlight smelled of musk and peppermint; although the day was warm, a lady carried a muff of panther-fur; she was followed by an Ethiopian in scarlet livery, bearing a letter sealed with Spanish wax. A naked child, an Eros cast in gilded bronze, drank from the sea-green shell of a melon, held high above his lips. Peter Innocent remembered that the Italians of an elder day, while yet that day was young, made melancholy synonymous with wickedness, and gave to the verb to "think" the sense of to "be sad." He took the meaning, but without a heavy mind; his heart's indulgence was poured like a libation over Venice and absorbed in her waters.

He remembered his old friend, the priest called Testa, the Diogenes of the spiders' webs, who shared his straw pallet with a familiar rat, and lived on mouldy bread and lentils. And he remembered, also, that other eccentric, the ancient with the iron bell, who was used to stand upon the quays and bridges, crying out with his own outlandish tongue and the bell's clapper, crying upon all men to be happy, in the name of God.

And although this person was a Moor and an infidel, he was nevertheless a philosopher and a lover of humanity. Peter Innocent thought of him with kindness, preferring him, perhaps, for a reprehensible moment, to the Christian priest, and wondering if he were not the wiser man. For Peter Innocent, flying through sunlight followed by a peacock's tail of foam, attired for once in all the splendour relative to his spiritual and temporal state, had not forgotten that long before he had assumed this purple he had fared very happily as one of the jongleurs of God. So, like the Moor, he rang continually a little bell whose tongue was not of iron, but of gold, and bright and silent as a flame.

The cardinal Peter Innocent was at all times silent, since Pope Clement had neglected to unseal his mouth; now he was hushed into a profounder stillness by his private felicity, and by the high and rapid speech of those about him. The Doge and the Procurator Manin were engaged in conversation with their illustrious visitor Pius VI; although preserving every indication of reverence for his Holiness, the Venetian nobles did not hesitate to address him with fluency and animation. The pope's nephew, the blond and arrogant Braschi Onesti, grandee of Spain and prince of the Holy Empire, stared somewhat haughtily upon these self-possessed patricians; he wore a coat of carnation velvet, and the little finger of his left hand was all but hidden by an emerald of fabulous value. At his knee the Abate Monti crouched like a beaten hound. "Consider the lilies—" and the pope's device, cut on a hundred monuments in Rome, was an heraldic wind, blowing down lilies like waves of the sea! This, too, was inscribed on marbles by Canova and the recovered classical remains of Herculaneum; yet Solomon in all his glory had no finer coat than young Braschi Onesti, nor could his seal have utterly outshone that green intaglio graved with the head of Agrippina. So thought Peter Innocent, and as the thought was, for him, faintly malicious, his smile flickered for a moment like a flame that has had a pinch of salt sprinkled upon its clarity.

For here, and suddenly, a small regret, an obscure discomfort, touched the cardinal with a pain no more important than may be inflicted by a kitten's ivory claw. So slight a blow it was that his mind scarcely recorded it; the glancing scratch cut the thin skin of his soul a little, as always, and if this same skin had been a visible thing, the closest scrutiny might have revealed a vast number of similar punctures, microscopically bleeding. This was the recurrent thorn in the clean flesh of Peter Innocent; this was his cross: he had no nephew.

So far as he knew, he was the only cardinal suffering under a like deprivation. He could not but consider the circumstance as a direct chastisement at the hand of God, yet he could not for the life of him decide wherefore the divine anger had so visited him; he examined his conscience, and found no really adequate sin. Nieces he had in plenty, the pretty flowering of Nicholas's romantic marriage; his sisters, having entered convents in early youth, might not, according to his code, be expected to serve him save by the efficacy of prayer. So far prayer had proved singularly inefficacious.

For his own part, he had prayed and fasted and made pilgrimages; there had been a period of hair shirts, but these had been forbidden by Pope Clement and his physician as merely a protracted form of torture of dubious virtue under the peculiar conditions.

Sometimes Peter Innocent wondered very vaguely and benignantly at the number of nephews possessed by some of the more powerful cardinals; it did not occur to his charity, however, to regard these youths as a commodity procurable by other means than the help of God and the wedded happiness of one's brothers and sisters. Of late he had been pricked to a certain reverential envy by the pope's very evident satisfaction in the society of the magnificent Braschi Onesti, haughty, negligently handsome, a prince of nephews indeed, and, more lately, a prince of the Holy Empire. Peter Innocent might himself have preferred a gentler nephew, a creature malleable and engaging to the affections of a mild old man, but at this moment he was immensely taken by the carnation velvet coat and Cæsar's signet-ring.

It is conceivable that he may have permitted himself a passing dream of parenthood—conceivable, but unlikely. The extreme chastity of his body extended to his spirit, or perhaps it were juster to say that the body and spirit of Peter Innocent was in this eighty-first year of his age a single amalgam, made from two substances of equal purity. This much is probable; that returning at a jocund season to a home of such miraculous loveliness as flowed and floated in the waves and clouds of Venice, he felt within the stiff and sanctified chrysalis of his flesh a lively movement as of uncurling wings, such exquisite and painted films as a moth hangs down to dry from the under side of a linden leaf. And he would have provided with joyous gratitude an opportunity to any saint to slit him down the back like a locust, if thereby might be freed a younger, fairer, and, to his humility, more perfect being than Peter Innocent Bon, perishing for this mystical offspring with all the fervour of the elder phœnix.

So thinking, or, more precisely, feeling, Peter Innocent passed into the monastery of St. John and St. Paul, whose venerable porch was a cavern dripping with refreshment after the full and golden glare of noon.

III: Ritorno Di Tobia

The next day dawned like a crocus, and all the lilies of the pontiff's suite arose in green and silver and vermilion.

Peter Innocent breakfasted on a large bowl of chocolate and a very small piece of *marzipan*, of which he was inordinately fond. The other cardinals sprinkled spices in their cups, or drank coffee sweet with sugar and brandy; they ate a great many little birds, roasted with bacon and red pepper, and they had strawberries from Passeriano and peaches from Algiers. Every one ate what he preferred; Braschi Onesti had candied chestnuts and champagne.

Presently the pope called Peter Innocent into his particular chamber. Pius was sitting up in bed; his beautiful ivory face looked grieved and weary under a canopy the colour of pot-pourri, heavy with a like perfume. Across his knees lay Sanazzaro's *Arcadia*, stamped with the dolphin of the first Manutius. At his elbow stood an engraved goblet of clear water.

"Peter," he said in a soft voice, "after I have received the Doge and the assembled signory and granted audience both public and private to various bishops of the Venetian territory, I shall be very tired. Yet, even so, I must assist, together with the Patriarch Giovanelli, at a *Te Deum* rendered by the voices of the ducal choir, accompanied by fivescore instruments under the baton of Pasquale Galuppi. I am ill; the journey has exhausted and the republic's arrogance annoyed a mind already languid with affairs. May I count upon your friendship to support me in this hour of trial?"

Peter Innocent was overcome by pity and amaze at the pope's condescension. He fell rustlingly to his knees, and picking up the pontifical slipper, which reposed upon a silken drugget by the bed, he kissed it with reverence. Pius smiled indulgently, extending his fine hand in a gesture of release to indicate a comfortable armchair plumped by pigeon-down. The cardinal regained his feet rather shakily and sank among these cushions, breathless.

"Holiness," he whispered, "what singular good fortune makes me capable of serving you, and in what essential does such service lie?" Privately, he prayed the business might not be connected with the Inquisition or the liberal opinions of his brother Nicholas.

"Merely this and thus," replied the pope, closing his eyes with an air of elegant fatigue. "This respectable choirmaster, Galuppi, has composed a cantata for five voices in my especial honour, and on the words of Gaspare Gozzi; it will be performed at the Incurabili this afternoon. Ludovico Manin pays for it, and it will be a very pretty compliment, but of course I cannot attend in person; the *Te Deum* will consume my extremest energies; my vitality can support no further burden. As the eldest prelate in my suite, you will make an acceptable substitute for the father of Christendom; as a Venetian, your presence will confer satisfaction, as, I trust, your sensibilities will receive pleasure; these men are your compatriots. May I rely upon you, my kind Peter?"

The cardinal was deeply touched by these proofs of confidence; he was also overjoyed at the prospect of hearing the musical result of a· collaboration between two beloved friends of his early manhood; he fancied he might meet them again and kiss their frosty cheeks. He had heard news of this cantata; its subject, the Return of Tobias, impressed him as being even more appropriate to his own obscure instance than to that of the sovereign pontiff. And he thought of the fresh virginal voices of the Incurabili, which had been taught to weave vocal harmonies as painstakingly as the fingers of less fortunate orphans are instructed in the intricacies of lace-making.

"Yes," he contrived to breathe, and "Gratitude," and "Holiness," and so was about to depart, when Pius stayed him with a gesture of white hands.

"Peter," he said affectionately, "if you are wearied by this ceremony, I will permit you to absent yourself from the festivities of the evening. Do as you please, my dear good fellow; you must have youthful affiliations to rebind, old memories to renew and cherish. I shall understand; this night is your own, unhampered by any duty to me. And, you know,—" he smiled very sweetly,—"a higher power is vested in my unworthy person; you may do as you like, Peter, for tonight, without fear of the consequences." His smile grew more indulgent, and he laughed with a peculiar tenderness as Peter Innocent kissed his scented ring and left him.

IV: Crystal Monsters

Blue dusk, thicker than fog and tinted with expressed essence of heaven along the falling colour of the dew, enveloped Peter Innocent as he slipped from the lighted doorway of the Incurabili; the music prolonged itself through other channels than his ears, and seemed to influence the hue of the most distant star and the perfume of the nearest pomegranate flower. He was happy, but a little loneliness, even a little fear, tinctured his mood. He had been unable to identify either of his old friends, and had found himself too shy to ask for them among the brocaded crowd of notables. Unobserved, he had sought the consolation of the twilight; he loved to be alone, but to-night his tranquillity had somehow failed him. He felt cold and rather tremulous as a touch fell upon his shoulder.

It was Alvise Luna, the glass-blower of Murano. He had grown very old, and his pale eyes were sunken in a face blank and dusty as a bag of yellow meal. Peter Innocent was shocked by the man's appearance, and greeted him sympathetically.

"Eminence," said Luna in a voice threaded by a whine, "I had not hoped to be recognized, nor, if recognized, acknowledged as an acquaintance by your Eminence. I have fallen upon evil times. I, whose ancestors worked in crystal for the great Duke of Buckingham and visited Tuscany at the invitation of the munificent Cosimo Second, I have not, to be frank with you, one copper coin wherewith to brighten another, I have drunk water for a fortnight, and the things I have eaten are not fit to be mentioned in your eminent presence. I am reduced to working for the infamous Giorgio Barbaria, who wishes to manufacture black glass bottles on the English lines; I have, as you may remember, considerable knowledge of foreign factories, and he pays me a dog's wages to instruct him. I am starving; my wife and children are starving; my little grandchildren are already dead from malnutrition. May I humbly beg your Eminence to aid me in my undeserved and dreadful trouble?"

This Luna was a liar and a sorcerer, and the Holy Office was already upon his path, which led through some of the most unsavoury cellars of Venice, marked out by a slimy brilliance like the track of a snail. But Peter Innocent did not know this, and had he known, he would not have understood it. He saw that the man was frightened, and he believed that he was hungry. As a matter of fact, Luna had plenty of money and merely wanted more; at the moment an enormous supper of polenta was distending his greasy waistcoat. But he was a dyspeptic, and his wry neck and hollow eyes looked wretched enough to move a more obdurate heart than Peter Innocent's.

"Of course," said the gentle old man, "of course, my poor friend, I will do what I can to help you."

An hour later, Peter Innocent was picking his slow, uncertain way down a damp and noisome corridor; Luna followed him, holding a candle as high as the dripping ceiling would permit. They descended a worn flight of stone stairs, and found themselves in a low-vaulted chamber whose debased Byzantine arches were dimly illuminated by a pair of ship's lanterns dependent therefrom.

This apartment was but too evidently a cellar, for a good three inches of water, cold and ambiguous, polluted the embroidered clocks upon the cardinal's stockings. Nevertheless, certain portions of the walls were covered by tapestries smouldering with the rich fancies of the Renaissance, and a number of carved cabinets and tables showed surfaces inlaid with brass or panelled in exotic lacquer. At one end of the chamber's secretive length, a small furnace filled with wood ashes made a spot of expiring rose-amber in the gloom.

Luna walked to the centre of the room, and, rapidly waving his guttering tallow back and forth, ignited in a flash a score of white wax candles cupped in coloured glass. Peter Innocent saw that a superb chandelier hung from the highest vaulting of the roof, a fantastic thing of flowers and icicles and silver bells, tinkling in the midst of squalor. And now, with a tinted radiance flooding every corner of the cobwebbed cellar, a hundred graceful and preposterous shapes sprang into the enchanted view: winged and maned and dolphin-finned, griffins and lions, stags and peacocks, and monsters fabulously horned and taloned.

The cardinal perceived in addition to these savage and exquisite creatures the accustomed implements of the glass-blower's trade: pontils and blowpipes, pincers and wooden battledores. Upon a platform, raised above the pervasive dampness of the stone-flagged floor, stood the workman's chair, with its rigid parallel arms suggesting some rude instrument of torture. Seated within this strange machine was a mysterious stranger, wrapped in a black cloak, and wearing a small mask of black velvet.

Peter Innocent at once became aware of an element of masquerade in the appearance of this person. Having himself long ago assumed a disguise, albeit an holy one, he readily observed the same quality in the dress of others, and as readily ascribed it to the most innocuous desire for privacy. He took the gentleman to be a person of simple and retiring disposition, and acknowledged courteously and at once Luna's gesture of introduction. The stranger rose, displaying an impressive figure, tall and muscular. He wore a quantity of beautiful lace, and his rings were diamonds of the first brilliance; save for these elegant details, his clothes were of a uniform sable hue. His head was covered by a short chestnut peruke, and through the slits of his mask his eyes glinted very dark and bright. The skin of his face and hands was swarthy and faintly lined; the cardinal judged him to be past his first youth.

"Your Eminence," said Luna in French, which he spoke fluently, having, for several disgraceful reasons, been much in Paris, "permit me to present M. de Chastelneuf, Chevalier de Langeist." The latter title was pronounced in the German manner, and the cardinal was at a loss to conjecture the stranger's nationality until he spoke. His manners were courtly, if a little antiquated and florid, but he conversed with a strong Venetian accent, and Peter Innocent had no doubt that he was a native of the republic.

The chevalier kissed the cardinal's hand with immense politeness, and began at once to speak of the prelate's poetical works, displaying a quite remarkable knowledge and acumen. In this way, and through the use of copious quotation from the classics, the gentleman contrived to convey an impression of learning and respectability, and Peter Innocent felt sure he must be a person of consequence.

Such, in a measure, was indeed the case, for M. de Chastelneuf, as this narrative must continue to call him, had at one time or another attracted the attention of almost every court of Europe, and on this very evening no less a notable than Messer Grand himself had given our gentleman much good advice not unconnected with the miasmic quality of the Venetian air, and the superior salubriety of Munich or Vienna. And since it was the chevalier's invariable habit to travel in a superb English carriage, emblazoned with the arms of a ruined lord, and as, moreover, he seldom travelled alone, he had been faced with the disagreeable necessity of selling his diamonds and his point d'Alençon without delay. Save for the fortunate intervention of Luna, who knew the cardinal's simplicity was good for at least a thousand sequins, M. de Chastelneuf might have been forced to part with his cross of the Order of the Golden Spur. It is not surprising that his happiness in greeting Peter Innocent was unfeigned and infectious.

Presently the cardinal found himself ensconced within the glass-blower's misshapen armchair, with dry slippers upon his feet, and a couple of hot bricks under these. A glass of excellent Levantine Muscat warmed his vitals; the long room appeared less cavernous, and the crystal apparitions which filled it glowed like jewels in the renewed stream of his own vivacity. His two companions were persons of wit and esoteric learning, and his admiration for Luna increased as he examined one by one the marvellous progeny of the workman's art. As for the chevalier, the delicacy of his mind was equalled only by its ascetic and fastidious grace: Peter Innocent was soothed and enraptured by this refined society.

The chevalier removed his mask, and his face showed handsome and aquiline, almost Oriental in its dusky tints, yet all Venetian in the liveliness and valour which informed its every smile. He had a nose like a falcon, and his deep-set eyes were black and gold. He told Peter Innocent that he had, in his youth, been honoured by the friendship of Benedict XIV, who had once taken his advice upon some little matters of no importance.

Suddenly M. de Chastelneuf rose to his very considerable height, at the same time making, for the benefit of Luna's eyes alone, an enigmatical sign whose nature it is impossible to describe. Luna also rose; the pair appeared to move in unison to some unheard and rhythmical injunction; salt and spices were destroyed upon the fire, and their smoke permitted to dim the purer radiance of the candle-flames. Then, at an unintelligible word pronounced by the altered voice of Chastelneuf, the incredible came to pass.

Peter Innocent beheld a golden griffin lift his wings to fan the air; a stag, of azure glass dappled with the same gold, stepped with a fairy pride across the expanse of

Chinese lacquer which separated him from his mate, and the two, meeting, caressed each other with delicate gestures of affection. A humming-bird, with feathers blown in pearl-colour and crimson, flew from his perch, alighting on the leafy chandelier; the spray that received him bent and swayed, and from its largest rose a petal drifted to the floor.

There is not the slightest use in pretending that Peter Innocent was shocked or even very greatly surprised. His mind moved happily in an atmosphere of miracles, and the charming nature of these phenomena precluded any suspicion of evil. He felt like a child who perceives at his first carnival a blue sky flowering with confetti, or who is presented at Christmas-time with one of those delightful German toys called Christbaum, bright with silver foil and tiny scarlet candles. So, without uncomfortable amazement, he stared enchanted at the delicious marvel of awakened life.

V: Piavola de Franza

It was Luna who finally crossed himself surreptitiously before addressing the cardinal in hoarse and lowered tones.

"Eminence," he whispered, "you have seen what our combined skill can accomplish; this, however, is only the beginning. It is very pretty to watch these insects and atomies, but what would you say to a flying horse able to transport your Eminence to Ecbatana; or a Cameroonian gorilla, blown in the best *mille fiori* and capable of strangling, with thumb and finger, persons inimical to your Eminence's peace of mind? I have, too, an extremely practical Indian serpent, the poison fang ingeniously supplied with *aqua tofana*." And he laid his hand upon the lock of a great chest, bound with copper, which occupied one corner of the room.

Peter Innocent turned pale as milk; in another moment he would have been constrained to believe evil of Alvise Luna. But Chastelneuf observed the old man's uneasiness, and stepping forward with an air of well-bred piety, he refilled the cardinal's empty glass and reverentially saluted his cold hand. Then he spoke very softly and persuasively.

"Monseigneur," he said, for despite his marked Italian accent he continued to employ the French language, "you must not be offended by the rough jests of my poor friend Luna; he is a stupid fellow, but good as bread, and of a simplicity truly pitiable in these wicked times. See how he has been persecuted by the Three, those sinister officials who deprived your noble brother of his liberty, and who have been the death of innumerable worthy citizens of Venice. Consider his industry, and talent, and then reflect upon his wretched circumstances and the sufferings of his devoted wife and children. I am sure you will consent to help him, Monseigneur; he asks no charity, but merely that you will patronize and encourage his beautiful craft by the purchase of one or two little articles of undoubted utilitarian and æsthetic value. This, for example—"

He made as if to open the iron-studded door of an inner chamber, but Luna stopped him with a clutch upon the arm and an imprecation. Chastelneuf smiled imperturbably and proceeded, flicking invisible dust grains from his satin sleeve:

"Your Eminence will graciously refrain from considering me presumptuous when I make clear the extent of our success in manipulating Murano glass; we are able to vitalize not only dumb animals, but even, with God's help, creatures formed in the divine image. It is a great responsibility, but I trust we acquit ourselves worthily as custodians of this sacred mystery. Monseigneur, you are ever in the company of the elect, but I, who am like your Eminence of a certain age, know all too well that the pangs of loneliness sometimes invade the most profoundly religious heart, and that our declining years, in their hallowed progression towards our Father's house, must needs require now and then the pitiful grace of human companionship, in salutation and farewell. If, then, the presence of a little being compact of modesty and sweetness, at once a daughter and a loving friend, blonde and ethereal as the ivory ladies of Carriera, could solace some spiritual hunger—"

He broke off, and silencing Luna by an imperious movement of the hand, walked firmly to the iron-studded door and opened it. Within, stiffly disposed upon a small gilt chair of French design, Peter Innocent could discern, though dimly, something like a large doll or a little girl; the creature appeared about sixteen years old, and wore a pale pink dress, trimmed with feather flowers in the best possible taste. A quantity of silvery-yellow hair fell to her shoulders, and her fair complexion was transparent and tinted like a shell. Her eyes were closed, her face tranquil and pretty. The cardinal was forcibly reminded of the Poupée de France in the Merceria, and, less vividly, of his sisters attired for their first ball, which was that given by the Morosini for Count Oldenburg in 1708, when he himself was six years of age. Since that time he had not particularly observed female clothing, except now and then in shop windows, and always rather to admire than to approve. He felt obscurely ill at ease, and although his heart was wrung by a certain air of pathos conveyed by the little figure propped on its gilded chair, he did not want to look at it any longer. He was distinctly relieved when Chastelneuf closed the closet door, which swung to with a ponderous clang of metal. Yet he was aware of a slight sense of cruelty towards the curious doll; it must be very lonely in the dark, behind the iron door.

"I should have no use, I am afraid, for

this interesting example of your art," he said somewhat timidly to the two men, who regarded him with scarcely concealed disgust in their veiled and greedy gaze. "I should really find myself at a loss to care for so complicated a piece of mechanism. The—ah—the young lady looks so alarmingly fragile, and I fear I do not understand the requirements of such—ah—such rarities. But I trust you will be careful to find a purchaser in whose kindness you can confide this poor—ah, child; she seems a mere child." He paused, interrogating them with his anxious blue eyes; they nodded in gloomy affirmation.

It is said by adepts, who may or may not be fitted to pronounce upon the subject, that when a man relinquishes the love of women from his infancy he condemns his predestined virgin to eternal violence wrought upon her by the demons of debauch. It is hardly reasonable to suppose that this young person artificially formed from Venetian glass can have suffered a like fate, but it is an unfortunate fact that Alvise Luna sold her, within the next fortnight, to an elderly senator of atrocious morals and immense wealth. He did not find her fabric durable, and perhaps she had no soul.

The chevalier was the first to break the

uncomfortable silence; he was at once his suave and animated self. The cardinal felt better immediately.

"I quite understand your scruples, Monseigneur," he cried with enthusiasm, and oh, how rare it is, in this material age, to discover virtue so sensitive or sympathies so warm as yours are proved to be! But surely, surely, there is some elegant trifle, some elfin toy, which might serve to remind you of Venice and of your youth within her occult circle of lagoons. A little greyhound, perhaps, or a talking parakeet; we have been particularly successful with parakeets."

At this instant the stupendous plan struck Peter Innocent like a falling star. He was dizzied by the glittering impact, and swayed in his chair, but his gentle voice was perfectly clear and steady as he answered: "Monsieur de Chastelneuf," he said, "and you, my old friend Luna, there is indeed something which I have long wished to possess, and with which your truly admirable skill may be able to supply me. Do you think, by any fortunate chance, that you could make me a nephew?"

Luna, who knew Chastelneuf to a hair's-breadth of precise disillusion, started in alarm as the other parted his smiling lips to reply; the glass-blower could have informed you to a semi-colon of the exact witticism fluttering upon the chevalier's tongue. To his overwhelming relief, the pungent butterfly was swallowed without the faintest grimace, and the words which actually emerged were models of chaste sobriety. A perfumed handkerchief passed across the mouth, the ghost of a sigh, and Chastelneuf's expression matched his speech. He was decorous, and only Luna knew the measure of his stoical abstention.

"Your Eminence," said the chevalier, bowing, "does us too much honour thus to admit us into a consultation on family affairs. But, happily, we are most excellently fitted to advise and aid you in this respect; we have, I may say, made a specialty of nephews." And he reminded Luna, with the toe of his buckled shoe, that a cheerful demeanour was indicated for this occasion.

Alvise Luna was more than a little troubled; he had not bargained for so extensive an order, and would have preferred to undertake a contract for a dragon or a Hyrcanean tiger any day. He was a religious man at heart, and although he was strongly predisposed by nature and inheritance towards chicanery and murder he viewed with profound distrust the extra-natural and Hermetic practices of his companion. To him there was something infinitely alarming in the idea of pre-empting the power of Deity to shape a being human at least in semblance, if not in soul, and he would rather have made a dozen manticores than one small baby. Nevertheless, he fixed his mind upon the heavenly shimmer of a thousand sequins, and entered with tolerable good grace into the current discussion.

VI: Aveeva Vadelilith

Peter Innocent had no difficulty whatever in obtaining from the pope full permission to absent himself for an indefinite number of hours upon the third night after the strange adventure just related. This latter night was that of May nineteenth, the date of official departure for the pontifical suite, but Pius bade the cardinal do as he pleased, and if he chanced to be too late to join the other prelates upon their leaving Venice, he might easily overtake them, said the Holy Father, during the journey of the following day, which must be made by water, and slowly, as befitted so illustrious a progress. He conferred his blessing upon the grateful old man, and, with the same indulgent smile, embraced him.

The season was Pentecost, and the water running in the veins of Venice appeared like wine under the transmutation of the sun. Pius VI, attired in the extreme of liturgical splendour, celebrated mass at the church of St. John and St. Paul. Passing out into the

Campo he imparted his benediction to the multitude from a high platform whose timbers were heavily overlaid with varnishes of gold. No sooner was this ceremony accomplished than Peter Innocent, his heart no longer a blue balloon, but a swinging censer of holy and aspiring prayer, hastened towards that equivocal quarter of the town in whose bowels the mysterious cellar lay concealed. He wore once more the indistinguished dress of a Franciscan friar, and as he walked, his eyes were fixed upon the pages of a little book whose covers bore the cruciform symbol of his faith.

Meanwhile Alvise and the Chevalier de Langeist awaited him in the vaulted chamber of their secret activities; Luna was observably nervous, but Chastelneuf was calm and majestic, the very picture of courtly self-possession in his coat of gold brocade and black velvet breeches, with a jewelled order tangled in the rich laces upon his breast.

"Rely upon my diplomacy," said this personage to his shivering companion. "I have learned much since the days of Mme. von Wulfe and the grand operation. I alone of all the adepts of my acquaintance have survived the wretched effects of Balsamo's petty larcenies. Saint-Germain is dying in Hesse, under the unpleasant pseudonym of

Zaraski. Cagliostro has incurred the rigours of imprisonment and poverty; he has abundantly deserved a severer punishment. I saw him first at Aix, in Provence, a mere boy, sewing cockleshells on his black oilcloth coat, while his young wife stood at his elbow, holding a great crucifix of some base metal coloured to resemble gold. She was adorably pretty, but depraved. That was twenty years ago, and I am wiser now; if my peculiar talents have languished, my judgement has ripened and matured. I am entirely satisfied with our preparations for to-night."

"That is all very well," sneered Luna, "but I have had all the hard work. My lips are cracked, and my hands flayed by such unexampled labours; I have performed prodigies; my lungs are old leather, and my windpipe scorched macaroni, yet you grudge me a glass of your precious *monte pulciano*, and I suppose I am to have a very dog's share of the money compared with your lion's portion. So it always is. Poor honest fellow that I am, I never manage to look out for my own interests, and yet I am the best glass-blower in the known world." And he began to weep in sincere self-pity.

"Quite true," said Chastelneuf, with careless good-nature, "and a lovely bit of work you've done to-day; your masterpiece, I cordially assure you. We could get an enormous sum for this juvenile Apollo from the director of the opera; he would make an ideal soprano, and both sexes would go into indiscriminate ecstasies over him if he appeared, shall we say, in the latest production of Cimarosa or Mozart? Of course I should have to alter my plans a little, but he should have a golden voice, I promise you. Only, I think our ingenuous prelate is, in the vernacular, the lucky draw in the lottery; he will not talk, and as he is by nature close-mouthed, he will have to pay through the nose."

"Are you determined upon waiting until after midnight to perform the undertaking?" asked Luna, with an anxious scowl. "I should have thought Thursday the more suitable date, and Thursday has yet three hours to run. Surely the thing you are about to do may be described as a political and religious operation; I have been reading your copy of Paracelsus, with its interesting marginal notes, and Paracelsus says very plainly that Friday is a day exclusively reserved for amorous works. I cannot see the connection, although it is quite like you to try to turn the most serious occasion into a common love-affair."

"Common, do you say?" cried the chevalier, indignantly. "*Cospetto!—Che bella cosa!* Is it a common occurrence in my life, I ask you, to refrain for three entire days from all human enjoyments, to confine myself to a vegetarian diet, and to eschew intoxicating liquors? A pretty regimen for a gentleman of my faculties! Then, too, I have had the trouble of burning, upon rising and retiring, a costly perfume composed of the juice of laurels, salt, camphor, white resin, and sulphur, repeating at the same time the four sacred words. I beg to remind you that I am no longer an amateur, as in the past; *Paralis* has advanced. As for the matter of the amorous operation, of course it is precisely that. Do you imagine I could send this poor innocent forth into the world improperly equipped to deal with his fellows? Friday it must be, or I'm a Turk!"

"As you please, as you please," grumbled Luna, resignedly. "I merely thought you might look very fine in a scarlet vestment, with a wreath of oak, poplar, fig, and pomegranate leaves; also I happen to have some ambergris, balm, grain of paradise, macis, and saffron lying idle about the place, which I understand are the correct perfumes for Thursday. But I was purely altruistic; for my own part I wish sincerely it were Tuesday, so that we might inaugurate an appalling work of vengeance. I fancy the blood-coloured robe and the magical sword and dagger. There is a beautiful picture of them in Paracelsus."

His face was alight with eager satisfaction, but Chastelneuf silenced him with a haughty sign of disapproval.

"Nonsense!" he said impatiently. "You know nothing whatever about it, and I advise you to keep your long nose out of such dangerous matters; these instruments of precision in the hands of the ignorant are lethal to the soul. Now, if you have prepared the inner chamber according to my directions, all is ready; but first let us have a look at the boy."

Luna could not suppress a grin of pride as he led the way to a heavily carved cupboard in the farthest corner of the room; the thing was a veritable cathedral in miniature, gothic and grotesque, with a hundred saints and gargoyles leaning from among its wreaths of fruit and flowers. He opened the door of this piece of furniture to a cautious crack; Chastelneuf peered over his shoulder. The two smiled joyously at each other as Luna closed the cupboard door with care.

"Miraculous!" shouted the chevalier,

slapping Luna on the back in a transport of enthusiasm. "Divine! And even now he seems to live: Alvise, do you know you have given him a distinct look of his reverend uncle: a sweet touch that; and oh, the delicacy of the thing! The hair, the eyelashes, the very finger-nails! O marvellous Luna!"

"It was a good thought that, to patronize your own tailor, though it has cost us a pretty penny," began Luna, handsomely, when a timid knock upon the outer door apprised the friends of Peter Innocent's proximity.

While Luna engaged the cardinal in more or less agreeable conversation, Chastelneuf disappeared into the inner apartment. The time passed rapidly, and Peter Innocent had just finished his third glass of wine and persuaded a pair of coral-coloured crystal love-birds to perch upon his forefinger, when the all but inaudible strains of a flute or violin recalled him from a waking dream. Guided by Luna, he passed into the other chamber, whence these sounds proceeded, and there beheld a scene of ceremonial enchantment.

Let it be clearly understood at once that the chevalier, whatever his peccadillos, practised only the higher forms of transcendental and divine magic, as opposed to nigromancy and goetia; otherwise he could have done nothing in the presence of such holiness as Peter Innocent's; the cardinal moreover carried upon his person a crucifix and a Book of Prayer, infallible talismans against the evil one. Here was no place for the Ahriman of the Persians, the Typhon of the Egyptians, the Python of the Greeks, the Croquemitaine, the obscene deity of the Sabbath. Let it be remembered that Isis was impeccable in her widowhood, that Diana Panthea was a virgin; that Apollonius of Tyana never yielded to the seductions of pleasure; that Plotinus of Alexandria was ascetic in the manner of his life; and that Raymond Lully was the victim of a hopeless passion which made him chaste forever. Vesper, not Lucifer, blazed now in the pentagram upon the marble pavement, and Peter Innocent stepped forward without fear.

The chamber, which was both larger and higher than the anteroom, was hung with charming tapestries of rose and green, and the chevalier was robed in vestments of sky-blue silk; a crown of violets encircled his chestnut peruke. His ring was enriched by a magnificent turquoise, and his clasps and tiara were of lapis-lazuli and beryl. The walls were covered with festoons of roses, myrtle, and olive, and the atmosphere quivered with the emanations of innumerable spices.

Upon the Parian floor there stood an altar of perfumes, and upon this altar there lay an unblemished lambskin, and upon this lambskin was traced in pure vermilion a pentagram with one point in the ascendant. It had been sprinkled with holy water, and dried by the smoke of myrrh and aloes, and over it Chastelneuf had uttered the names of the five genii, which are Gabriel, Raphael, Anael, Samael, and Oriphiel.

The adept towered above the tripod of evocation; he bore in the centre of his breast a copper talisman with the character of Anael traced thereon, together with the words: "Aveeva Vadelilith."

Luna withdrew into the shadows, where he waved slowly an enormous fan of swan's feathers.

VII: Conjuration of the Four

Peter Innocent came forward into the light, which fell with an effect of moonshine from the sacred lamp. He had no sense of fear and, what is more singular, no sense of sin; this appears to be indisputable proof of the beneficent quality of the ritual employed by Chastelneuf, upon this occasion at least. The cardinal never told of that night's wonders, and had he done so he would certainly have been burnt by the Holy Office; but his conscience remained immaculate throughout. He had his private theories, however, concerning the Christian and supplementary ceremonies proper to the undertaking, and he held his book and his crucifix very firmly in his two hands as he confronted the chevalier.

Chastelneuf lifted in the air the true and absolute magic wand, which must not be confounded with the simple divining-rod, or the trident of Paracelsus. This was composed of a single perfectly straight branch of the almond-tree, cut with a golden pruning-knife at the exact moment of its flowering;

one of the extremities was fitted with a triangular prism, and the other with a similar figure of black resin; this end of the wand was gilded, and that silvered. A long needle of magnetized iron pierced the entire length of this consecrated instrument, which was the verendum of the magus, too occult to be shown to uninitiate eyes; the chevalier was probably unwise to employ it in the presence of the cardinal and Luna, but he was a brave man, and very vain of his attainments.

"As this creature to whom we are about to impart the privilege of living is composed of natural elements, I purpose to invoke the spirits of these components, which are the Four: air, water, fire, and earth. He who is about to be born was formed from sand and holy water, fused in extremest heat and shaped by human breath. Through the agency of these powers, a spirit shall enter into this bodily image, but whether mortal or elemental I cannot tell, nor does it greatly matter."

Chastelneuf spoke thus with an authentic dignity, which deepened as he proceeded with the exorcisms. And now the cardinal perceived behind the altar an object of funereal character, resembling a bier; it was covered by a white cloth whose folds conformed in some measure to the outlines of a corpse decently disposed for burial. The thing had been invisible a moment since; now the rays of the lamp were concentrated upon its ominous quiescence.

Tracing their symbol upon the air with an eagle's quill, the adept now intoned the prayer of the sylphs; he exorcized the water by the imposition of hands, and by mingling with it a little consecrated salt and the ash of incense. The aspergillum used was formed of twigs of vervain, periwinkle, sage, mint, and basil, tied by a thread expertly abstracted from a virgin's distaff and provided with a handle of hazelwood from a tree which had not yet fruited. The prayer of the undines was then recited with proper solemnity, and afterward the prayer of the salamanders, so soon as the fire had been suitably exorcized by the sprinkling of salt, white resin, camphor, and sulphur, and by calling upon the kings of the sun and lightning, the volcanoes, and the great astral light. Lastly, the earth was exorcized by efficacious means, and the gnomic prayer pronounced. The chevalier then lifted successively the sword, the rod, and the cup, and proclaimed, in a loud voice, the conjuration of the Four.

"Caput mortuum, the Lord command thee

by the living and votive serpent! Cherub, the Lord command thee by Adam Jotchavah! Wandering Eagle, the Lord command thee by the wings of the Bull! Serpent, the Lord Tetragrammaton command thee by the angel and the lion! Michael, Gabriel, Raphael, and Anael! Flow, moisture, by the spirit of Eloim! Earth, be established by Adam Jotchavah! Spread, firmament, by Jahuvehu, Zebaoth! Fulfil, judgement, by fire in the virtue of Michael! Angel of the blind eyes, obey, or pass away with this holy water! Work, winged Bull, or revert to the earth, unless thou wouldst have me pierce thee with this sword! Chained Eagle, obey my sign, or fly before this breathing! This, by virtue of the Pentagram, which is the morning star, and by the name of the Tetragram, which is written in the centre of the cross of light! Amen."

At this moment the white cloth covering the body seemed to move of its own volition, rising slowly until it floated free of the bier; its corners were drawn apart, and the fabric violently divided into four quarters. Upon a narrow trestle Peter Innocent saw the figure of a young man; he appeared very tall and slender in his complete immobility. He was dressed in the fantastic extreme of fashion, and his costume was the more singular in that it was entirely white. He wore a white velvet coat embroidered with silver spangles, a velvet waistcoat to match, white satin breeches, white silk stockings, and shoes with diamond buckles. His linen and lace were exquisite, and on one hand was placed a curious ring consisting of a large crystal set over white satin.

The cardinal stared intently at the face of this elegant creature, but could distinguish little save the suggestion of a straight nose, arched eyebrows, and the glimmer of pale hair over a paler brow. The eyes were closed, the hands relaxed and quiet.

Meanwhile, above the tripod, the mystery thickened with the perfumed smoke; there came a loud command, a moon of radiance appeared, dissolved, and vanished, and with the most startling celerity the young man bounded from his couch and gracefully abased himself before the venerable prelate, in whom he seemed to recognize a father or a friend. At the same instant the chevalier stepped forward and affected an introduction between the two, mingling simplicity with polished ease of manner.

All were visibly moved by this happy consummation of their ritual, and even Luna permitted a few tears of relief and cupidity to trickle down his dusty cheeks. Chastelneuf was laughing, shaking hands, and offering choice wines in slim Murano goblets to the cardinal and his nephew. The boy smiled, bowed, and sipped with the most lifelike gestures of politeness; but Peter Innocent stood silent in a tranquillity like stone, bewitched and awed by his felicity, and gazing at his nephew with infinite love and wonder in his eyes.

VIII: Creature of Salt

Upon the most minute examination, Peter Innocent failed to discover anything in the appearance of his young kinsman—for as such we must henceforward consider him—which could suggest an abhuman origin or composition. True, the boy's skin was so fair as to seem almost translucent, and the luminous flax of his abundant hair had the fragility of spun glass; but these details merely served to give distinction to his undoubted beauty. It is possible that Luna had employed, in weaving with his breath these miraculous lovelocks, a secret method by which his ancestors had produced *vitro de trina*, or crystal lace, of such spider-web delicacy that it shattered at the vibrations of an angry voice or the too poignant wailing of a violin. The long gold eyelashes matched the hair; the eyes themselves were the colour of sea water, the pure Venetian aquamarine.

As opposed to the very ornamental lightness of his physical equipment, the young man's manner was composed and firm, and his perfect self-possession might have contained a hint of patronage had its affability been less pronounced. He ignored Luna with charming good-humour, condescended to the chevalier without offending him, and put Peter Innocent at his ease with equal facility and despatch.

"My dearest uncle, my more than father," he cried with fastidiously restrained emotion, saluting the cardinal on both cheeks with the utmost tenderness, while two bright glassy tears, volatile as quicksilver, fell shining through the air. "Chevalier, that's a sound wine, though heavy to my particular fancy. You don't happen to have such a thing as a *viola de gamba* about, do you? A little music would not be amiss,—I am sure you sing,—that sweet duet of Cimarosa's, let us say." And he began to hum, in an enchanting tenor, the words:

"Prima che spunti
In ciel l'aurora . . ."

The cardinal put out his hand, and softly touched the white satin sleeve of his new nephew.

"Dear boy, it gives me the greatest satisfaction to witness your careless happiness," he said timidly, "but there is one thing, one slight precautionary measure, which I hesitate to omit, much as it grieves me to interrupt your singing. I wonder if I might trouble you for a little clear water?" he continued, turning to Luna with a courteous smile.

The chevalier bounded forward, eager to serve, with the stoup of holy water from the evocative altar; but Peter Innocent shrank hastily away as he shook his silver head in refusal.

"Not that, I think, my kind friend. Believe me, I am very grateful, but if I might have only a cupful from the spring which I observed in the adjoining cellar, I should prefer— Ah, you are goodness itself; I thank you."

Peter Innocent took the water which Luna brought him in a cracked china cup; holding it very carefully, he blessed it according to the Roman ritual, thus establishing its potency against evil spirits. This was a different consecration, indeed, from that surrounding the furniture of the chevalier's altar; this blessing, uttered in the old man's quiet voice, was spoken with another and an holier authority.

". . . that wherever thou art sprinkled every phantasy and wickedness and wile of diabolic deceit may flee and leave that place, and every unclean spirit. . . ." Thus was exorcized the creature of salt lurking invisible in the broken cup, and likewise the creature of water . . . "that thou mayst avail to uproot and expel this enemy with all his apostate angels, by the virtue of the same our Lord Jesus Christ."

Now was the water become a creature in the service of God's mysteries for the driving out of demons. In a whisper so low as to be well-nigh inaudible even to the boy, who at a sign had knelt upon the pavement with instinctive docility, Peter Innocent repeated certain formulæ of blessing especially efficacious against devils and invocative of divine protection. Clear drops of water fell upon the bowed and shining head.

Chastelneuf was secretly annoyed.

"That was quite unnecessary, I assure you," he said rather stiffly. "There is not an ounce of harm in the boy; the prescription calls for the purest ingredients, as Luna can tell you, and, for my own part, I have used the best magic known to the ancients. However, as you will. I suppose we all have our prejudices."

"I was sure you would understand an old man's anxiety," replied the cardinal, pacifically. "And now I will not trespass longer upon your kindness, save to give you this little wallet with my profoundest gratitude, and to wish you both a very good morning."

It was morning, and between the cracks in the jalousies pale blades of light were driven like angelic swords.

"Where are you taking the boy, Eminence?" asked the chevalier with renewed cheerfulness, playing a lively tune upon the jingling wallet, whose chorus was five thousand sequins. "Remember, he's scarcely used to a rough world as yet, and his finger-nails may be brittle for a day or two."

"We are going to the Church of St. John and St. Paul, my friend, where this poor child must receive the sacrament of baptism," Peter Innocent said slowly. He looked with pity and something perilously near adoration into the smooth, transparent countenance of the boy, who clasped his arm and smiled in meek response.

Mounting a short flight of steps, M. de Chastelneuf flung open an iron-barred door, and suddenly dawn flooded the room like a river of golden water loosed upon it. Without, the canal still preserved a sleepy colour, neither grey nor blue, but the house-tops were painted in extravagant tints of rose and flame by a sun new-risen from the Adriatic.

"What name will you give the boy, Monseigneur?" inquired the chevalier. "I feel a certain proprietary interest in his fortunes, which under your auspices must be uniformly happy, and I should like to know his name."

The cardinal mused, considered, and replied.

"I believe I shall call him Virginio," he said, his eyes tracing the exquisite and ingenuous outlines of his nephew's half-averted face.

"A pretty name, but I trust it may not long be strictly appropriate; I have spared no pains to make our young friend a complete work of art, after the best natural patterns," answered the Chevalier de Langeist, with a not unpardonable pride, bowing deeply as Peter Innocent and his pale and luminous companion passed into the morning, and so were gone like a black pearl and a white, melting within a chalice of honeyed yellow wine.

END OF BOOK ONE

Book Two: VIRGINIO

"I had had an affair with the moon, in which there was neither sin nor shame."

—Laurence Sterne.

BOOK TWO: VIRGINIO

IX: Of Sappho Little, But All Roses

IN Angelo Querini's classical garden at Altichieri there stood a summer-house dedicated to the goddess of Folly; this charming structure was, paradoxically enough, presided over by a bust of Marcus Aurelius and decorated with a motto from Montaigne. A more apposite taste had graced the dovecote with a Grecian Venus, and raised an altar to the spirit of tranquillity in the midst of abundances of sweet basil, lavender, and thyme.

Midway between an Egyptian sarcophagus and an Etruscan monument, both heavily overgrown with deep viridian moss, a marble bench disclosed its rosy veining to the September sun, and seemed to invite a languorous repose in keeping with the season. From the door of the shadowed summer-house a young girl presently emerged;

her lively glance surveyed the autumnal lawns and arbours, and instantly selected the carved and coral-coloured seat as most benignant to her mood. She carried an armful of books; these she disposed within reach, herself reclining in the sunnier corner of the bench. She was soft and inscrutable as a Persian kitten.

A black kitten among the bright and gilded trees, with hazel eyes transfused with gold, and hair so dark that only at the temples a darkening golden tinge survived in smoky black. Her dress was black as soot; such a dress, decent, and austere, as clothed Querini's admired and admirable young friend Fulvia Vivaldi in her Genevan retreat; too black, in spite of the clear muslin kerchief and the silver chain, for Rosalba Berni on her eighteenth birthday.

This was, then, the celebrated Rosalba, better known among the Arcadians of Italy as Sappho the Younger, or to the more affectionate few, the Infant Sappho. This child was an orphan by report, and by profoundly proven faith the ward and adoptive daughter of the noble and liberal Angelo Querini, ex-senator of the Venetian patriciate and valued comrade of Voltaire. It was openly declared that she was a descendant of Francesco Berni the poet, to whose sparkling blood she owed her marvellous wit and the inventive lightness of her mind; other more insinuating murmurs attributed these qualities to an equally effervescent source: the whispered name of the Cardinal de Bernis was a veritable Arcadian diploma of mental grace, and Rosalba's eyebrows were distinctly French.

She had these brows, arched forever in a delicate amazement, drawn upon a smooth forehead; her dark hair grew in a point; and her eyes were large between black lashes; their expression was calm, but impertinent. Her mouth was curled like a scarlet petal in some early frost of irony; her skin was white as the rose of her baptismal name. Across her slightly tilted nose a score of golden freckles made her human; for the rest, in form and elegance of gesture, she was Artemis.

Yet not the Artemis of ivory or of quarried stone, however exquisite. Rosalba was more vital than opening roses or ripened fruit; she lived and moved and burned within the chilly greenery with a palpable warmth; she was a flame whose consummation may be bitter, but whose promissory blooming is tenderer than apple blossoms. To the five senses of an observer she was indeed imagined flowers to breathe, as she must have been velvet to touch, cream to taste, the crescent moon to gaze upon, and, to the listening ear, a melody repeated by a mocking-bird.

It was all to the credit of M. de Chastelneuf that the five senses of this particular observer were so poetically acute; the young Virginio leaned upon a mossy column, while love for Rosalba Berni whirled over him like a fragrant wave, and left him drowned in those same waters from which the mother of such love arose.

" 'O bianca Galatea!' " said Virginio, politely, quoting Metastasio.

"My name is Sappho," Rosalba replied rather crossly. "I do not care for Italian verse; I prefer the classics, and, above all, Ossian. I am at present busy, very busy, with a translation of the latter, for the benefit of those unfortunate people who are unable to read it in the original Gaelic."

"Is it not written in English?" Virginio inquired timidly. "And have I not heard that Signor Cesarotti—"

"Be silent, if you cannot converse intelligently."

Rosalba pronounced these words with perfect calm; she was imperial rather than rude.

"Precisely," Virginio returned, with a gentle smile; she was suddenly aware that he was far more beautiful than any Adonis in Querini's garden. He reminded her of marble. Or was it marble of which he reminded her? Something more translucent; crystal, perhaps.

"I am reading, as you see," she said more kindly, "but I can spare you a few moments; I dare say you would like me to show you the books I have this very morning received from my kind friend and guardian. Approach, young sir; the gate is unlocked, and if you will wear white shoes, you must expect the dew to spoil them."

Virginio drew near her as one who visits, in simple reverence and awe, the shrine of an immortal; she laughed, and made a place for him beside her on the bench, among the richly bound volumes which surrounded her.

"Here, my poor boy, are the 'Confessions' of Rousseau; I suppose you have never read them. For my part, I have been familiar with their pages for years; this rose-coloured levant is merely a new dress for an old and adored companion. Here, is the 'Cecilia' of Signorina Burney, published this same year in London; it will be so much Greek to you. Here is some real Greek; a manuscript copy of the Codex Palatinus, or Anthology of Cephalas; the original is unfortunately locked up in the Vatican library."

"Where could it be safer, or in the company of so many equally holy treasures?" asked Virginio in mild surprise, which turned to actual terror as Rosalba whirled upon him with the silken savagery of a little panther. It was now evident that, whoever her father, her mother must have been Italian.

"Are you a victim of superstition, and dare to enter these sacred shades?" she cried in honest indignation. Her eyes were burning amber, and the crisp tendrils of her hair appeared disturbed and shaken. Virginio trembled; a faint cracking sensation menaced his expanded heart.

"I am a Christian," he contrived to enunciate; he was very pale, and looked more than ever transparent. Rosalba was touched in spite of her convictions.

"Do not be distressed; I am myself a deist," she cried generously. Virginio put his cold hand over his sea-blue eyes; bright glassy tears fell into the air, and lay like silver on the yellow linden tassels at Rosalba's feet. "My poor boy, we have all made mistakes," she told him, seriously; she found his emotion curiously disturbing. "Look, I am often very silly myself; I have wasted half my birthday morning in re-reading a peculiarly childish novel by Carlo Gozzi. I am ashamed to admit that his fairy-stories have always had an attraction for my mind. Listen; it was this that I found so absorbing, this nonsense." And she proceeded to read the following passage from a shabby little book bound in coloured paper, and furnished with a marker of green silk ribbon.

"'A lady, adorned in the Venetian fashion, with a Florentine petticoat, and a blue satin vest, apparently fresh from the mercer's, trimmed with sleeves of the finest lace; she wore rings and bracelets of the richest gold, and a necklace set with Indian diamonds.'"

X: Poesy Ring

Rosalba's voice died into quivering silence; she hung her supercilious head, and the contemptuous petals of her lips parted to sigh. "The 'Cecilia' was given me as a special concession to feminine frivolity; it may also serve to improve my English," she murmured with apparent irrelevance. "It is a delightful book, I am sure. And next year I am to have the Encyclopédie, if I am diligent. Has not my dear Jean-Jacques a beautiful new dress, the exact shade, would you say, of a pink geranium?"

Virginio's shining flaxen brows stirred faintly to a frown.

"Would you not prefer a beautiful new dress for the adornment of your own divine beauty?" he inquired with respectful interest. "I do not think a geranium pink coat particularly suitable to the charms of M. Rousseau."

"Oh, but I would rather have yellow," cried Rosalba, in spite of herself—"Pale yellow like a frosted leaf, or rosier, like the sunny side of peaches."

She stopped, sincerely sorry she had not been inventing pretty images for a poem about philosophy or the ringlets of a child. Shame tinted her cheek more delicately than imagination can contrive to colour it. Virginio's veins were molten with love and pity.

As a matter of stern, immutable fact, Rosalba was hardly a fit object for pity, although love enveloped her in a natural shower like sunlight. In the Venice of her time, and indeed throughout the whole of Arcadian Italy, she had from her precocious childhood been petted as a tenth and darling Muse; flattery had been her painted rattle, and early fame her skipping-rope. Yet since no visible laurel had enwreathed her hair, and since her dress was sombre with decorum, Virginio saw not Sappho, but Cinderella.

A blush suffused Virginio's face; the blood showed clearly, like wine that stains a pearly glass. From his hand he drew the curious ring which the Chevalier de Langeist had given him. It was a large crystal set over white satin; the band was gold, engraved with an English motto.

"Will you accept this trifling gift upon the fortunate occasion of your natal day?"

he asked, with a graceful inclination of his luminous head.

"Yes, and most gratefully," Rosalba replied, with a smile of simple pleasure. "This is precisely what I have longed to possess; this must, I think, be an Indian diamond."

"Nearly, but not quite," Virginio admitted. "However, it is, as you see, very singular and charming; that is magic written on the gold. The words are possibly in cabalistic Hebrew; I know at least that they are secret and in the highest degree potent for conjuration."

"That is not Hebrew; that is English, I believe," said Rosalba, pondering the inscription. "It says—but this is extraordinary—it says, 'Fear God and love me.' The sentiment is elevated, and the language extremely choice; the whole forms an appropriate motto for a deist."

"The first words, yes; these are intended for the deist," explained Virginio, who did not have the slightest conception of the meaning of this mysterious term. "The rest—that enchanting phrase, if I may be permitted to repeat it; that legend, 'Love me,' this is addressed to the woman, the goddess, the eternal, unattainable Diana. Accept the prayer; put on the ring, O loveliest." He affixed the bauble, with a kiss upon her middle finger, where it hung a little loose; it had fitted his own slender ring finger to perfection.

"I shall give you a guard," he said, "a guard of Indian diamonds." Rosalba laughed for joy.

"Touching the comparatively unimportant matter of my presence here to-day," Virginio continued suavely, retaining, with an air of negligence, Rosalba's hand within his own, "I must explain that I bear a letter to the noble Angelo Querini; it is upon the part of my revered uncle and benefactor, Cardinal Bon. These two were comrades in their season of tender youth; their hearts preserve the innocence of that vanished aureate age. My uncle desires to intrust me to the occasional kindness of his friend; he hopes I may be now and then allowed to visit Querini in his hallowed seclusion. I require, it seems, a certain amount of rustic air; my constitution is unfortunately fragile." Virginio did his charming best to appear pathetic, and succeeded admirably in the attempt; against the light his lifted hand moved in a crystalline transparency.

Rosalba frowned at the name of cardinal, but Virginio had already learned to prefer a frown to a smile in such an instance; as a cardinal's nephew he was accustomed to many and repellent smiles upon inimical lips. He was rather grateful to the girl for her look of gravity; it was his profoundest wish to be taken seriously, and persons of both sexes were but too apt, in his brief experience, to credit him with a mental lightness commensurate with his physical mould.

"Why are you not in Rome?" Rosalba questioned somewhat accusingly. Her manner revealed fastidious distaste, and Virginio was deeply grieved by her intolerance.

"I am too ignorant as yet for Roman society," he said quietly. "My uncle has arranged for my education at the Academy of Nobles in Venice. The age of admission is only eleven, but I am very simple-minded, and, besides, nobody can be certain of my exact years. I have, for my own part, a strong conviction that I am not less than nineteen and not more than twenty."

"I should say you were tall for nineteen and remarkably silly for twenty," Rosalba answered cruelly. Then, as he stood silent and very pale, she put out her hand again and touched his fingers in impulsive pity. Her hand was warm and vibrating with life; Virginio's hand was cold and thin, and as she clasped it, an ominous cracking startled her with strangeness, she felt as if his fingers were so many brittle icicles.

"Be careful, Signorina; you may injure yourself," said Virginio, sadly, examining his hands with the minutest care.

Rosalba looked at her own palm, where a tiny scratch showed scarlet; she could have sworn that a splinter of glass still clung there. Suddenly she was afraid; she stared at the boy in an enchantment of horror. The sun shrank up into a savage polar star, and the heavens were another colour than blue. The trees had tongues, and when she shut her eyes, she could hear the shuffle of their heavy feet upon the protesting grass; its blades were presently to be reborn as serpents.

Then two bright glassy tears, volatile as quicksilver, fell shining through the disfigured day, and as they splashed upon Rosalba's little breast, she drew Virginio beyond her fear and comforted him in the security of innocence.

So, with the utmost simplicity, Rosalba Berni was constrained to fear God and love Virginio all in the space of five seconds, yet this thing, so quickly done, was not to be undone within the memory of that generation, and when the dark and the flaxen head were frost and silver, the event remained unchanged.

XI: Calmon the Philosopher

"I trust that the noble Angelo Querini will approve our engagement," said Virginio in a tone of practical good sense, after a brief and iridescent cloud of unreality had enveloped them for a time in silence, whose mist dispersed too soon. "I think we should hasten to make known to him the history of the past fifteen minutes; he has been as a father to your girlhood, and he should be told of our betrothal without delay."

"H-m," and "M-yes," replied Rosalba, doubtfully; she was not certain that she wished to be betrothed; still less did she desire to acquaint her noble guardian with a fact so subject to the alterations of fancy. "Oh—shall we?" she inquired with a notable lack of enthusiasm.

"It is our duty." Such was Virginio's obdurate opinion; Rosalba accepted it, to her own surprise and considerable indignation. Dimly, as an inauspicious providence perceived through wizard crystal, she began to be aware that her lover was incapable of bending, however cruelly a clumsy world might break the refinement of his substance. In a prophetic flash she realized that she must henceforward and always, as the ancient Venetian proverb has it, handle him with white suède gauntlets steeped in rose-water.

Gentle and grave, and by her footfall half reluctant, she passed from the sumptuous autumnal sunlight of the garden into the chilly corridors of Querini's country house; the floors were paved in lozenges of grey and yellow marble, and upon the walls a long procession was frozen in magical decay, which had once issued like a rainbow from the fresh and glittering palette of Carpaccio.

At her side Virginio stepped delicately and very proudly, in shining contrast to her austere black silk and bloodless lawn; he wore his white satin coat with silver spangles, and the lace upon his shirt might almost have purchased Constantinople from the Ottoman princes.

To Angelo Querini, in his pillared library, frescoed in faintly gilded russet and religious blue, and presided over by a bronze bust of Lord Verulam, the boy was an apparition from the fabulous other side of the moon.

This impression was the more amazing, in that Angelo Querini believed in neither apparitions nor fables save as the results of an imperfect digestion and an inferior intellect. His was a mind so purely rational that it had long since demanded and received absolute divorce from his naturally impetuous heart, which was thereby set at liberty to be as affectionate and foolish as it pleased without disturbing in the slightest degree Querini's mental conviction as to the profound selfishness of all human action. In this way his head was enabled to breathe the invigorating airs of philosophic disgust, while his heart enjoyed to the full a lifelong orgy of benevolence; Minerva might have sprung from his reasonable brow, but the daughter of his breast was Charity.

Therefore it was a foregone conclusion that the liberal cynic would overlook the irregularity of Virginio's birth, and the kind old man receive him as a son. Rosalba, until this moment free as a humming-bird nourished at the Muses' hands, felt the meshes of a sudden net envelop her in its invisible gossamer. Being herself a philosopher, she reflected sagely that the disquieting fact of her capture being now quietly accomplished, there was no further wisdom in revolt. Besides, in her innermost soul she no longer desired a freedom vacuous of Virginio, and as she took her guardian's congratulatory kiss, she succumbed for the first time in her life to the warm, delightful luxury of complete unreason.

In this delicious mental condition, she listened ravished to Virginio's account of his supernatural origin; neither the boy's simple confession nor Querini's kindly satirical smiles disturbed her in the slightest degree. Personally, and counter to every conviction which had so far upheld her brilliant intellect, she was inclined to credit her lover; but the whole question appeared to her of trifling importance compared with the exquisite grace wherewith Virginio expounded it, and she cared very little whether he had emerged from an Arabian orange or flown to earth upon the wings of the celebrated Green Bird, so long as he had come to her at last.

"This is a romance worthy of the invention of your friend the Count," said Querini, answering her thought. He was benignant, he was even tender, but Rosalba recognized the sceptical amusement in his eyes. She blushed, then blushed again more vividly, ashamed of blushing.

"The Count must be right, after all; this story, of whose accuracy I can entertain no doubt, must prove him right," she said firmly, opening her own eyes very wide in a glance of calm and arrogant assurance. No longer need she conceal her predilection for fairy-tales, nor fear to admit that her favourite author was, after all, not M. Jean-Jacques Rousseau, but Count Carlo Gozzi. Magic was justified by experiment; it was become a verity, true, rational and possible, like mathematics or the rights of man.

It is regrettable to be obliged to confess that the noble Angelo Querini did not share Rosalba's belief in Virginio's narrative; he felt quite certain that the handsome youth was the blue-eyed flower of Peter Innocent's wild oats. It is to the credit of his heart, however, that he viewed the supposed offspring of the cardinal's folly with the most solicitous compassion and respect. His mind emitted a private spark of laughter, reflected in his eyes, perhaps, but admirably absent from his grave and courteous lips.

"Curious, curious indeed," he ruminated gently, while joining their hands with a logical deistic blessing. "These little ones are the children of superstition and vice, yet how powerless has been the error of their parents to infect their intrinsic loveliness! Oh, nature, virtue, reason, and Voltaire! Oh, excellent Helvetius! Philanthropically bestow upon these infants a ray of your own illumination! May their bodies remain pagan, their minds emancipated, and their moral qualities incorruptibly pure!" In his excitement he had almost pronounced "Amen," but caught himself in time to substitute a sentiment from the "Republic" of Plato.

XII: Uncles and Sons

At this very moment, by one of those pleasing coincidences more common in romantic fiction than among the ineptitudes of mortal life, the Cardinal Peter Innocent Bon, Count Carlo Gozzi, and the Chevalier de Langeist sat together within a turret chamber of the haunted palace of Saint Canziano; upon the countenance of each gentleman there brooded an expression of thoughtful melancholy. The lofty room, open to the four great azure winds of heaven, was festooned with cobwebs and dustily strewn with the count's famous collection of Arabian and Neapolitan fairy-tales. These volumes, in many instances richly bound in ancient levantine leathers, were fallen into a state of sad decay, repeated in the person of their owner, who had worn the same wig for twenty years, and whose silver shoe-buckles were broken. The door drooped upon its hinges, the window-panes were starred and splintered, and from the carven ceiling enormous spiders dangled mockingly above the absorbed faces of the three friends.

It can occasion no undue surprise to learn that Peter Innocent and Carlo Gozzi had been comrades since boyhood; the saintly and fastidious prelate and the aristocratic dreamer were spiritual kinsmen from their hereditary cradles. It is not generally known to history, however, that the patrician Gozzi and the adventurer Chastelneuf had even the slightest acquaintance with each other, and indeed it was the invariable care of both to conceal the circumstance; nevertheless, a sincere affection existed between them. It is possible that this mutual esteem was the result of a certain pamphlet, lampooning the Abbé Chiari, of which the chevalier was the reputed author. Such rumours had cost him dear in the opinion of the Council; they had, perhaps, rewarded him with the singular friendship of Carlo Gozzi.

Chastelneuf was splendidly attired in ashen-grey velvet; a silver-laced hat, a furred travelling-cloak, and a small white mask were flung upon a lamed and tattered chair at his elbow. Peter Innocent wore his severest habit; the slight disorder of its austerity suggested another journey, less luxurious than the chevalier's. Gozzi had wrapped his emaciated form in a ragged dressing-gown, apparently constructed from a bit of tapestry, in which the loves of Leda and her swan had been decently terminated by the sempstress; a virtuous pair of shears had shortened the fable with the garment, and left both the count and Leda colder for their loss. Two senatorial portraits by Titian and Tintoretto ignored the goblin chamber and its occupants with respective airs of proud detachment and opulent contempt.

"I had hardly expected to find my worthy —ahem—my interesting friend M. de Chastelneuf a member of our little company, Carlo," said Peter Innocent, timidly. He disliked very much the prospect of hurting any one's feelings, but he had come all the way from Rome on purpose to consult with the count upon matters of secrecy and importance; the chevalier's presence was a glittering blow to privacy, while his suave voice delicately divided silence, as one cuts a precious fruit. The cardinal, very kindly, wished him in Vienna.

Chastelneuf glanced at the count with smiling eyes beneath lifted brows; the latter answered the unspoken question at once.

"My dear Peter," he cried rather impatiently, "do you suppose the chevalier has travelled post from the Austrian frontier, and that at the gravest danger to his personal fortunes, for no better reason than to interrupt our consultation? On the contrary, it is he who shall resolve our difficulties; he has an excellent plan, and one which cannot fail to meet with your approval. But first let me ask you; did you furnish this vitreous young relative of yours with letters of introduction to Angelo Querini?"

"I did, without doubt," the cardinal assured him plaintively, "and at the cost, moreover, of several severe pangs of conscience. Querini is an estimable person in many respects, and my brother Nicholas was devoted to him. I cannot forget, however, that the man is an unbeliever and a Voltarian; he has insulted holy church upon various pretexts; he is a mocker and, I am afraid, a confirmed philosopher."

" 'Mock on, mock on, Voltaire, Rousseau!' " muttered Carlo, who had seen the poem in manuscript among the papers of an eccentric English scholar of his acquaintance. " 'And the wind blows it back again!' Where it listeth; true, very true. A detestable person, Querini; he cultivates plaster busts in his garden, which have devoured all the elves. But Chastelneuf says he has a pretty niece, a nymph by no means plaster."

The chevalier permitted himself to smile slightly in replying.

"Not a niece, my dear Count; a ward is surely another matter."

"Why?" demanded Peter Innocent with unwonted asperity; as an uncle, he resented the implied sneer without understanding it.

"Ah, Eminence, spare my blushes upon such a question!" Chastelneuf cried gaily; an impudent and evasive laugh puzzled the cardinal by its refined ribaldry.

"Do not quarrel, gentlemen," protested Gozzi, who was deriving a wicked satisfaction from this curious encounter between the powers of light and semi-darkness as represented by his friends. "We are all met today in order to discuss the future of two ingenuous young creatures in whom I, for my part, take the warmest and most fatherly interest."

"Two young creatures?" The cardinal looked pale with alarm. "Did I understand you to say two, my dear Carlo? Virginio has never been, so far as I know, anything in the least like twins."

"There is no question of twins, save in so far as the sweet affinity of lovers may simulate the natal bond," began Carlo Gozzi, but the chevalier interrupted him with something less than his customary politeness.

"Of course there can be no question of twins as yet," he said in a low, shocked voice, turning upon the cardinal a face congealed into dignified horror. "We are barely arrived at the point of arranging a match between Virginio and the niece of Cardinal de Bernis, and already your Eminence is talking of twins. The thought is perhaps a little indelicate, although we may all indulge such hopes in the intimacy of our devotions. But as to the match, is it not exquisitely suitable, and can you possibly withhold your approval when I explain—"

"Marriage! Virginio married!" exclaimed Peter Innocent, wildly; and, "Bernis! The niece of Cardinal de Bernis!" cried Carlo Gozzi with an almost comparable accession of surprise. "I thought he was going to study the Greek dramatists!" added the one, while the other ended, "And I, that she was the ward of Angelo Querini!"

XIII: Spiritual Fathers

"You were both quite correct in your conclusions," the chevalier reassured them.

"The divining crystal upon my watch-chain informs me that Virginio has this moment opened a folio of Sophocles, while the noble Querini is giving the best possible proof of his benevolent guardianship by conferring a double blessing and a modest competence upon the betrothed pair; his notary has but just entered the room; I believe he is about to draw up a new will. It is all very charming and idyllic, and I congratulate your Eminence most heartily upon a felicitous solution of your problems." He bowed, nor could the cardinal detect a look or gesture indicative of aught save urbanity and good humour.

"My problems were, after all, very simple, and you should not have come all the way from Vienna to solve them, Chevalier." Peter Innocent hoped he was not speaking too haughtily to this adventurous person; Carlo Gozzi healed whatever breach the gentle voice had made by laughing cynically and wiping his eyes upon a large bandana handkerchief. It was impossible to say whether he was merry or sad.

"It was all my fault, Peter my dear," said Carlo Gozzi. "I have been melancholy of late; I miss my poor Truffaldino and his company of masks. In parting, we embraced, weeping bitterly. I had not wept since that mischievous lunar moth, Teresa Ricci, flew away to the moon where she belonged, but now I cannot stay my tears. In vain have I attempted to be philosophical, which is merely to say heartless; my hopes have perished with the venerable comedy of Venice, which I must soon follow to undeserved oblivion. Meanwhile my one comfort has been the society of your delightful nephew; in him I have renewed my youth and experienced afresh the enchantment of fairy-tales and the ravishing pleasure of the impossible. I visited him in the sombre Academy of Nobles. In his black uniform, enveloped in a bright blue cloak, he was precisely like one of the disinherited princes of my own fancy; I loved him, and I longed to see him happy."

"I know you have been goodness itself to the boy, my Carlo; he wrote me of lessons in Arabic and antique Spanish. He cannot have been lonely in your edifying society, and now with these new excitements and adventures in the classics into which Querini is about to introduce him, his days will be overflowing with aureate dreams indeed. What more can the lad desire?"

"Don't you understand, Eminence?" asked the Chevalier. He gazed sternly at the cardinal, while true and generous indignation kindled within his smouldering golden eyes. His sinewy brown hand had sought and found his sword-hilt before it fell, still clenched, in recognition of Peter Innocent's silvered and benignant locks. "I beg your Eminence's pardon if I appear impetuous, but the boy, the poor boy, is, after all, very nearly human."

"Oh, I trust he is not merely human," interposed Gozzi. "There has been some talk of elementals, and I have always longed to meet an elemental. Virginio, with his translucent flesh, like flame made frost—Virginio is happily something better than human, or so I have believed."

"And is there something better on this inferior side of heaven?" Chastelneuf spoke with passion, and yet there was a perilous tenderness in his falcon look.

"We are all of us God's children, and fashioned in His image; we are moved by a breath of His divinity," said the cardinal, softly and somewhat fearfully; but Carlo Gozzi was not satisfied.

"Did you or did you not, M. de Chastelneuf, assure me, upon your honour as a gentleman, of this youth's supernatural origin?" he demanded hotly. "I have loved him like a son, because I conceived him to be magic incarnate; am I to learn now that he is a common mortal like myself, and perhaps of baser clay?" He stared significantly at the chevalier, and his words were a challenge.

"Oh, no! Oh, no!" said Chastelneuf, wearily. "Calm yourself, my dear Count; your suspicions are unfortunately unfounded. The boy is all that you could wish him to be; he is an exquisite monster, a celestial prodigy, blown from the very air itself, and captured in an earthy net so fragile that its meshes could not withstand the violence of a mortal soul. I do not know to a certainty what spirit informs this mutable fabric; whether it be a creature of the elder world, nourished in the heart of a sapling or fallen from between the breasts of a cloud; only I think it lacks the roughness and the pitifulness of humanity. Be content, both of you; the cardinal may have his angel and the count his elfin prince; Virginio will never disappoint you. I have given him a ring;

the same was given me in my youth by a beloved friend, and its influence is infallibly benign. If it should chance to light a little fire in that hollow heart, and set true tears burning in those glassy eyes, such marvels are not harmful, but salutary and kind. I, too, have felt for Virginio an affection fatherly and apprehensive; I have come from Vienna for the express purpose of promoting his happiness, and it is my prayer—yes, my profoundest supplication to my Maker—that this happiness is about to be consummated."

He fell silent; to Gozzi, who knew him well, it was an amazement to perceive a veritable moisture dimming the vehement colour of his eyes.

Peter Innocent was moved; his countenance, placid and humane as a sacred effigy, was turned toward the Chevalier in lenient concern, as Chastelneuf sat down and covered his face with his hand, shaken by some curious fit of ardour or revolt.

"I will consent to any plan, within reason, which can promote my nephew's ultimate happiness," said Peter Innocent, gravely.

Chastelneuf still bit his lip in tormented silence, but Gozzi burst forth into voluble rejoicing as he wrung the cardinal's hand with warmth.

"Oh, good! very good indeed! This is the best news I have heard in a twelvemonth. Peter, I knew I could rely upon your merciful heart when you were made to realize the boy's loneliness and isolation; Chevalier, my compliments to your invariable sagacity. Oh, it will be an extremely charming little romance, a fairy-tale come true, not desiccated and compressed within the pages of a book, but alive and kicking its scarlet heels, as the ancient Bergamesque proverb puts it. And the lad is actually a fantasy in Murano glass instead of vulgar flesh and blood! I myself could not have invented a prettier conceit, or one more gracefully in accordance with the best magical traditions."

Peter Innocent observed this enthusiasm with indulgence, but a natural anxiety led him to seek further enlightenment from his friend.

"And who, pray, is the young lady whom I am about to embrace as the bride of Virginio and, consequently, my own child? If I am not mistaken, the chevalier described her as a niece of Monseigneur de Bernis."

"Oh, niece if you like; that title does as well as another," said Chastelneuf, with recovered sprightliness. "And, indeed, I honour your scruples; nothing is more lamentable than lascivious gossip and scandal-mongering. But in this case, it can do no harm to admit what your Eminence, as a man of the world, must already have suspected, in view of a certain prelate's profane reputation; the fact, in fine, and to make a long story short, that this lovely girl is a daughter of Cardinal de Bernis and . . ."

"But must you make it short, Chevalier?" interrupted Gozzi. He made no effort to conceal his eagerness, and his wintry eyes were bright with anticipation. "Your stories are always so entertaining, and never too good to be true; I am sure that Peter will join me in urging you to continue at your leisure with the recital of this mysterious amour. Eh, Peter, my boy, are you with me?"

XIV: Nuns and Lovers

Peter Innocent, whose eyes were blue as veronica flowers, and whose inmost soul was as a silver reliquary of chaste design, felt somewhat at a loss to conjecture whether or no he was, precisely, with Carlo Gozzi at the immediate moment. A doubt, insidious and sinister, as to the exact nature of the company filtered between the argent filigree of his reflections; he smelled brimstone as the count opened his tortoiseshell snuff-box, and observed with relief the normal outline of the chevalier's elegantly buckled shoes. When he replied, his speech was tempered by unaccustomed caution.

"Carlo, I cannot quite say that I am with you, but I hope I shall never be very far from such an old and trusted friend; no difference can sever us that may not be bridged by a clasp of the hand. Only I wonder a little. Is it, was it, entirely suitable for Cardinal de Bernis to have a daughter?"

Gozzi appeared slightly embarrassed, but

Chastelneuf assumed the responsibility of answering without a trace of hesitation.

"Monseigneur, I feel sure your fears will be set at rest when I explain this affair; its complete suitability is perhaps its chief charm to a refined mind. The Cardinal de Bernis was possibly, in his youth, faintly inclined towards profligacy; he was brilliant and well bred, but flippant and occasionally unwise. Some of the ladies upon whom he bestowed his butterfly favours shared his weakness; one alone of all that rainbow number remained modest and virginal even under the intoxication of love. I knew her; it might have been my privilege to preserve her delicate illusions from maculation at the hands of beasts. She was unwavering in her faith, which, most unhappily for her, was pinned not upon the bosom of her God, but starrily, like a bright religious order, over the shifting heart of François-Joachim de Bernis."

"Proceed," said Gozzi. "This begins to be amusing."

"The tale is not truly amusing," said Chastelneuf, meditatively. "It is sad, I am afraid, and its only happy ending is Rosalba, who is herself not an end, but a beginning. For the French ambassador at Rome it is very sad; for a little Venetian widow it was, perhaps, sadder. I will tell it to you, if you like, but I cannot promise to make you laugh except at the ridiculous spectacle of my own tears."

"Go on, my friend," replied the inscrutable Gozzi. Peter Innocent was silent, but from an inner pocket he drew a fine cambric handkerchief, sweet with lavender.

"I am the villain of this piece, Eminence," the chevalier continued with a sort of melancholy pride. "When I have finished, you will find it impossible to condemn Bernis; your feelings towards the innocuous partner of his unwisdom can be no harsher than regret softened by commiseration. Ah, Caterina, if I had never led you into that select conclave of libertines, you might even now be a happy wife and mother, and I, content and honoured, the father of a lovelier creature than either Virginio or Rosalba! I may say without vanity," he added, "that in my youth I was not ill favoured."

"Proceed! proceed!" cried Gozzi, impatiently. "You were always as black as a Moor; Time has spilt no milk and roses from your leather cheek, over which you should waste your tears. Be good enough to stop crying, Jacques; tell your story."

"It is now nearly thirty years since I first saw Caterina," Chastelneuf went on. "She was but fourteen years old, and her little face had all the blameless brilliance of a child's. I loved her, but with a levity and cynicism incomprehensible to my maturer perceptions. I seduced her, but tenderly, for I had determined to make her mine legally and for life. We spent hours in the gardens at Saint Blaise, where we ran races together; the prize, which I permitted her to win, was a pair of blue garters. I was captivated; her candour, her ingenuousness, her vivacity, all contrived to make me her slave, for the union of beauty, intelligence, and innocence has ever swayed me.

"A parent, perhaps no crueller than her lover, but certainly for the moment more severe, immured Caterina within a convent at Murano; we were unable to meet, and had only the chilly comfort of smuggled letters, and the ambiguous tremors of hope, as sustenance for our reciprocal dreams. I gave her my portrait, commissioning a young Piedmontese to render it in the smallest miniature; he painted an exquisite Saint Catherine of the same dimensions, and a clever Venetian jeweller mounted them both in a ring. The patron saint concealed my countenance, but the expert craftsman had provided the fantastic setting with a hidden spring, and I fear that my pictured eyes often disturbed the devout eyelids of poor Caterina by hot and secular tears.

"This comedy continued for several months; I grew very thin and mournful, and lived miracles of faithfulness in the mere denial of my natural instincts. At last I made bold to enter the convent chapel; one of the novices was about to take the veil, and I knew I might pass unobserved among the crowd of visitors.

"After the investiture I walked into the convent parlour with the other pious spectators, and standing within four paces of my poor little love, I perceived her gazing at me in a species of ecstasy; happiness made wide her hazel eyes and parted her lips to suspire tenderness.

"Alas! I had no sooner conferred the fleeting joy of my smile upon this unfortunate child than I robbed her again, and forever; my heart, always elastic, rebounded from the small and shrinking form of Caterina, to fall with terrific violence at the feet of a tall nun beneath whose cool reserve a secret fire was visible, even as her coif disclosed an unlicensed curl of red-gold hair above a face fair to pallor and lovely to delirium. I was completely overcome; my head swam among singing clouds, and I should assuredly have fainted had not a kindly old lay sister led me into the sharp sea winds of the conventual garden.

"If ever I write my memoirs, which I shall refuse to call confessions, since that infamous rascal Rousseau has profaned the title, I may describe at leisured length the course of my infatuation for the nun, Mary Magdalen, and its legendary end; I may aspire to draw her portrait, more intimately even than my young Piedmontese drew it for me, naked upon a couch of black satin, demure and shameless behind an ivory medallion of the Annunciation fitted into the lid of a gold snuff-box.

"This refulgent lady was the friend of the Abbé de Bernis; she had taken the veil out of pure caprice, and had the discretion to conceal any unhappiness she may have felt. Her illustrious birth and her extravagant liberality procured innumerable privileges denied to the other nuns; the tale of her amorous adventures must not insult the laudable ears of your Eminence. Suffice it to say that she and I between us plotted to debauch the peaceable simplicity of poor Caterina; I gave my darling to the power of the dog, and in a room of mirrors, lighted by girandoles and candelabra of rock crystal and gilded bronze, Bernis took the child in his arms and drank her frightened tears with feverish avidity. I retired, laughing, to sup with Mary Magdalen in the adjoining chamber; the nun was disguised as a handsome youth in rose-coloured velvet and black satin, and we devoured oysters and truffles from silver chafing-dishes and fine Dresden china. The wines were burgundy and champagne; I remember that I was excessively thirsty. I was mixing a salad of anchovies and hard-boiled eggs when the door opened and Bernis entered, followed by Caterina.

"Bernis was a man of forty; to my intolerant eye he was already a little worn, a little thin; his good looks were faintly tainted by effeminacy. He was invariably dressed in the extreme of elegance; the beauty of his hands was proverbial.

"Now, with an air of the most polished courtesy, he offered one of these miraculous hands to Caterina; he bowed, and I saw nobility rise to his forehead, shaking back the perfumed flippancy of his thoughts as a lion shakes back his mane. So I knew that although I had abandoned my darling to the lion, the power of the dog was dead. I am ashamed to admit that I was furiously jealous of Bernis.

"I cannot tell you the truth of this matter because I have never known it. What I conceive to be the truth seemed inconceivable at that confounding moment; the room, with its vain and equivocal elegance, its exquisite depravity, its engravings by Meunius and Toletana, the lovely epicene figure of the nun, the perverse integrity of the ambassador's bearing, all conspired to render the scene incredible. Caterina, attired in a childish gown of green gauze, was composed and smiling; she looked up at Bernis, and her gaze was limpid with faith. I was very angry; knowing a portion of my loss, I raged inwardly, and longed to kill the two; the deeper significance of their mutual glances was hidden from my eyes by a curtain of blood."

XV: Came Forth Sweetness

Peter Innocent had covered his face with the lavender-scented handkerchief, but Gozzi remained satirical and unmoved. The chevalier brushed the back of his hand across his shining and dilated eyes, as if to dissipate the remembered darkness of crimson. He continued to speak in a measured and deliberate voice:

"I did not see Caterina again; she returned to the convent at Murano, and within the year her parents had married her to an honest Venetian lawyer, who adored and tormented her youth with an intolerable devotion. Bernis, as you know, was soon afterwards recalled to France; the nun Mary Magdalen and I were left to console each other with meditations upon infidelity. Our natures were but too similar; each libertine despised the other, and we parted without regret or charitable illusion, without prejudice, and without compassion for each other's spirits, subdued to such resemblance by the unloving flesh."

"Peter, if you can make, as the peasants

say at Chioggia, either dragon's head or mermaid's tail of this unholy rigmarole, you are a cleverer man than I, and that I should be sorry to believe!" exclaimed Gozzi in exasperation, as the chevalier's recital drew to an apparent close on a note of profound repentance.

Peter Innocent raised his seraphic and bewildered eyes, enlarged by tears too scorching to be cooled by a cambric handkerchief; he did not look at Gozzi or at Chastelneuf, but straight into the sky, a deep, blue pool reversed, suspended, spreading like a tree, like a shade, like the shadow of a sapphire rock.

"I can make neither head nor tail of this tragedy, Carlo," he answered, "yet, for my comfort, the chevalier has made me believe it has a heart, and that not chimærical or devilish, but vulnerably human. I cannot understand, and yet, beneath the covert and obscure, I can feel the beating of a heart."

"You are a cleverer man than I, Peter," said Carlo Gozzi, who believed in elves. He said it in humility, for sometimes he believed in angels.

"You are right, Eminence; it is the heart of poor mortality which beats in my story, and echoes in your ears; the sound is the sum of human hearts which still vibrate in unison because, though broken, they have mended each other with love."

Chastelneuf spoke solemnly, but Gozzi questioned him with a quizzical scorn.

"Do you say love, O melancholy Jacques?"

"I say it," replied the chevalier; the habitual visor of insolence masked his face upon the word. "To clarify the matter further for your Eminence's comprehension," he went on, in a light and cursive voice, "I must remind you that Bernis had no sooner become a power in France than he had the unfortunate honour of incurring the enmity of the royal favourite. He had the temerity to suggest that the Prince de Soubise was not a fit person to command the King's armies; the Pompadour was majestically offended, and when the pope presented Bernis with a cardinal's hat, Louis bestowed it upon him with his own hands and forthwith exiled him to Soissons, where he remained for six years, a broken and embittered man."

"Lorenzo Ganganelli loved that man," said Peter Innocent.

"I know he did, and therefore his successor hates him, Eminence; when you return to Rome, you may do a kindness to a dying lion."

"Chevalier, I think you are wrong; I am

very old, and I should only weary the Cardinal de Bernis," Peter Innocent replied modestly.

"Your nephew's sweetheart will not weary him," Chastelneuf cried with a curiously happy laugh. "Wait; do not believe me a madman. I have more riddles to elucidate if you can spare me the patience."

"I have a fabulous appetite for old wives' tales," Gozzi admitted rudely, and Peter Innocent was quiet and kind in his silence.

"Good," said the chevalier. "We were at Soissons, were we not? At Soissons in a cold December, with a northeast wind and seventy miles dividing it from the classic gaiety of Versailles. Here, among Gothic churches and darker mediæval memories of Saint Crispin the Shoemaker and Louis the Pious, here where Becket prayed and Abélard despaired, Bernis came alone and sorrowful, having put his trust in princes, and served his country better than his king's mistress.

"Imagine, if you are something kindlier than stone, the desolation of that Christmas season, when in Soissons the Gothic roses of Notre Dame were carved in snow, and the Cardinal de Bernis sat alone in his vast apartment. He had caused no fire to be lighted, no supper to be laid, and when the chimes, like stars made audible, began to pierce the midnight with rejoicing, he stopped his ears against their voices, and wept the burning tears of Lucifer fallen from heaven.

"At that moment, out of the darkness, upon the wings of the bells as it were, and feathered with snow like a little bird, Caterina came to him."

"Thank God!" said Carlo Gozzi, fervently. Peter Innocent said nothing.

"She folded him in her grey cloak, that was all feathered and furred with the snow, and she kissed his beautiful cold hands. It was the first kiss she had ever given him; she gave it to the lion who had delivered her from the power of the dog, at Venice, in the room of mirrors, on an evening of full carnival, when she was only fourteen years old."

"I am glad she came," said Carlo Gozzi, adding, after he had cleared his throat, "I suppose, then, that we are to understand that Rosalba Berni is the offspring of this interesting union!"

"Yes, you are to understand precisely that, my dear Count; I fear you are incapable of fully appreciating the poignancy of the situation, but the bare facts you are at liberty to understand," answered the chevalier with impudent urbanity. He finished the tale, turning his blazing eyes towards Peter Innocent, who continued to say nothing.

"When Caterina came to Soissons on Christmas eve, she was seventeen years old and a widow. At that time Bernis was past forty, and tired by the vanities of a Dead-Sea dream, an ashy-flavoured world. Six years later, when Rosalba was born in the South, her father could laugh very lightly as he sprinkled her with almond blossoms and peach blossoms and cherry blossoms or tickled her lips with a pigeon's feather. Perhaps he was happy because he had been recalled to court, where he had magnificently rejected the seals of office; perhaps he was happy because he was archbishop of Albi. Perhaps, on the other hand, he was happy because of Rosalba, who had been born in happiness in the South, in a farmhouse whose outer walls were covered with espaliered peach trees, and whose windows were fringed with climbing roses. Upon the day of her birth a golden peach knocked at the door and a white rose flew into the window. Bernis ate the peach and gave the rose to Caterina. To the child they gave the name Rosalba.

"At Albi, the archbishop's palace is a fortified castle of the Middle Ages, and perhaps it is not strange that Bernis loved better the farmhouse with the espaliered fruit-trees. Here for five years a golden age endured; a little world existed for a time, round and smooth and perfect as a peach. A bitter stone was hidden in its heart, but before Bernis set his teeth to that his felicity was absolute. Then, in the plenitude of summer, Caterina died.

"Bernis gave every rose in the garden to Caterina; she clasped them with gentle indifference. In this same manner she accepted his last kiss; he was glad enough to go to Rome, to assist at the conclave which elected Lorenzo Ganganelli. He had a chill conviction of her forgetfulness.

"Rosalba was conveyed to Paris in the care of an impoverished cousin of her father's; this gentlewoman was amiable, but frivolous and injudicious. Having acquired a little wealth through the generosity of her kinsman Bernis, she repaired to Versailles, taking the child with her. There, in the midst of that sumptuous, but effete, civilization, Rosalba was remarked by Madame Necker for her wit and beauty and selected as a playmate for that lady's precocious little daughter.

"Thus, while yet of tender years, the girl was made free of the best *philosophe* society;

by the time she was twelve she was among the shining ornaments of Madame Necker's Friday receptions; the Mondays of Madame Geoffrin, the Tuesdays of Madame Helvétius, were incomplete without Rosalba's elfin grace. Her cousin desired above all else a fashionable marriage for her protégée but beneath brocaded petticoats the child's silk stockings, though gossamer and clocked with lace, were already obstinately blue. She refused, by impertinent implication, a round dozen of silver-gilded youths; Versailles was a blown Easter egg, excessively sugared, and she cared only for political reform and the awards of the Académie française."

XVI: Diversions at Ferney

"Intolerable imp!" exclaimed Count Carlo Gozzi in disgust. "It is this same horror, this unfeminine baggage, this most ungentle lady whom I have laughed to scorn in all my charming plays! She is the Princess Turandot, who utters riddles in the tone of an academician; she is Barberina, who has read Holbach while Carletti was dressing her hair. I had hardly realized the extent of her folly. However if you, Chevalier, say she is pretty—and you do say so, do you not?"

"And good? You have assured me of her virtue?" faltered Peter Innocent.

The chevalier regarded them with skilfully displayed contempt; he elevated his eyebrows the polite fraction of an inch.

"Eminence," he pronounced, "it is even possible, as the French pastry cooks have it, to put too many perfect ingredients into a pound cake. Enough, they remind us, is better than dyspepsia. Yourself and the count may live to regret the fact that Rosalba has never had a cold in the head or an illaudable impulse. Such things are, perhaps, disfiguring for the moment, but they humble the spirit of the young. Rosalba is not humble."

"Is she proud?" said Peter Innocent.

"Not in the least, Eminence," Chastelneuf replied. "She is merely perfect. You may be completely at ease in her company; she has the simplicity of the truly great."

Carlo Gozzi snorted indignantly, but Peter Innocent perceived no cause for annoyance. His simplicity excelled Rosalba's.

"And her friendship with Voltaire?" he went on a little nervously in spite of the chevalier's reassurances. "I have wondered, do you know, whether that were quite desirable. Of course its results were most fortunate; there can be no doubt that Querini has sheltered her from every tempered blast. But Voltaire as the intimate companion of a child of twelve—no, I confess the reflection has troubled me."

"Monseigneur, as I said to M. de Voltaire after reciting thirty-six stanzas of that divine twenty-third canto of 'Ariosto,' describing the madness of Roland with the most dreadful accuracy,—when I had finished, I assure you, the philosopher fell upon my neck, sobbing; tears were in all eyes,—but, I repeat, as I said to him at this affecting moment, you are too satirical, *cher maitre;* be human, as now, and like Ariosto you will be sublime! Oh, I remember it very well! Your Eminence is right; there was a vein of irony in the man which I must be the first to deprecate. And yet, he had intelligence; I think Rosalba was attracted by his intelligence. Then, too, you would not have her guilty of ingratitude, and he was kind to her."

"He stole her from a convent, did he not?" inquired Gozzi, who was beginning to be bored by the continued amiability of his two friends. To his relief, Peter Innocent looked shocked; the chevalier remained incurably good-humoured.

"Oh, quite!" the imperturbable chevalier cried. "But such a convent! Really, I cannot, in your Eminence's presence, attempt to explain; there were, however, circumstances too distressing to recall. I should hardly go so far as to say he stole her; rescue is the appropriate word, surely. The affair was shrouded in mystery; some said she had been immured by her ambitious cousin for refusing to wed a one-eyed marquis; others that she had incurred the enmity of the Neckers by embracing the free-trade principles of Turgot. Still another version, and that which I am myself inclined to credit, ascribes her abduction to the machinations of a rich Englishman, Milord Camphor or Camphile, who returning widowed from the East, beheld and desired, within the chilly inspiration of a single breath, Rosalba's loveliness and warm vivacity. It is but natural that the squire of Ferney, who had heard all of these stories in their most exaggerated forms, should have hastened to free this adorable creature from the chains of tyranny and vile superstition."

"And the name of this convent?" asked Peter Innocent, rather apologetically.

"That, Eminence, I am not at liberty to divulge; another time, perhaps. You see," the chevalier added, "it was the same convent from which M. de Voltaire had previously rescued Philiberte de Varicourt."

"Oho! Belle et Bonne!" exclaimed the count, who evidently saw. Peter Innocent did not, but his modesty prevented him from demanding an explanation.

"Precisely. And here, very luckily for little Rosalba, our good friend Querini appeared upon the scene. He came to pay his last respects to Voltaire; the fatal journey to Paris had already been discussed; 'Irène' was well-nigh completed, and the patriarch experienced, within his venerable breast, a lively and determined longing to visit once more the country of his birth. The noble Angelo Querini found the household at Ferney more or less at sevens, elevens, and thirteens, as the school children say; Rosalba was crying in the boot closet under the stairs, and 'Belle et Bonne' was biting her nails in her boudoir. M. de Voltaire and the Marquis de Villette were locked in the study drinking English punch and suffering from profound depression."

"What had occurred to disturb their philosophical serenity?" asked Gozzi, with an air of quiet satisfaction.

"Nothing; nothing at all, save that the Sage of Ferney had committed the trifling indiscretion of addressing Rosalba as 'Plus Belle et Plus Bonne' in the fascinating presence of Philiberte. Our little friend had just completed a very creditable Horatian ode, entitled 'To My Heroic Champion'; this she recited, wearing a neat new frock of dark blue merino, with her hair arranged in becoming ringlets. The result was curious, and, to a man of eighty-four, disturbing. I have sometimes suspected that his decease was hastened—but, no, these ladies' dainty and frangible shoulder blades must not be burdened by so deplorable an event as the death of Voltaire! He perished of a surfeit of coffee and academic honours."

"Unrepentant," said Carlo Gozzi with intense and pleasurable conviction.

"Perhaps merely discourteous," said Chastelneuf, kindly.

Peter Innocent said nothing; he was absorbed in silent supplication for the immortal soul of François Arouet de Voltaire. The Deity's replying silence appeared to him an unconditional consent to his request for leniency. The softened airs and mistier hues of the Venetian afternoon surrounded this moment with a mild halo of salvation, and Peter Innocent felt sure that the sage was forgiven.

Far away, across the melancholy marshes of Altichieri, Virginio and Rosalba, fantastically cloaked and masked, had seized the same propitious moment to ascend the steps of the chevalier's elegant English carriage. They bore a large portmanteau and a couple of bandboxes, and the noble Angelo Querini, as he slammed the emblazoned door upon their smiles and blushes, wished them Godspeed with all the prayerful emotion of his foolish heart, while his sagacious brow condemned them for a pair of young lunatics, whirling in spangled frenzy towards a riddle and a doom.

END OF BOOK TWO

Book Three: ROSALBA

"But some, and these the elect among gardeners, will always prefer China Roses."

—Christopher Warren.

BOOK THREE: ROSALBA

XVII: Golden Bride

"AND now," murmured Chastelneuf with obvious regret, gazing dreamily over the housetops, which the descending day had diapered with a changed and more intricate design of shadow—"and now, I repeat, my patient friends, there is little left to tell. You have been indulgent; the hour grows older, and matures into a time more suited to adventure than to these vague reminiscences. In a word, Querini adopted Rosalba upon the spot; he conveyed her to Venice, and encouraged her in the study of the arts and sciences. Poetry was her natural voice; the Arcadian Academy received her with acclaim, and forthwith fell down and kissed the abbreviated hem of her schoolgirl's gown. The Infant Sappho was baptized in Castalia, and shaking the fountain drops from her juvenile curls, she lifted up her throat to sing. The rest you know; it cannot take me above five minutes to recount the principal events of Rosalba's Venetian career. You must remember—"

"But is it quite necessary, Chevalier?" Gozzi inquired with plaintive scorn. "We have all heard too much of the Infant Sappho; some of us, impelled no doubt by morbid curiosity, have even read her verses. We recall very vividly and with peculiar pain the ridiculous festivities which marked her coronation at Rome, and all the nauseating verbiage, which, with the bad luxuriance of a weed, has kept her reputation virulently green. If you desire to converse further about the past, I must beg you to confine yourself to your own memories; why not favour us with an account of your escape from the Leads?"

Chastelneuf smiled; he was well aware of the count's savage irony, but he turned to Peter Innocent with bland composure.

"If his Eminence wishes; I am always at his disposal."

"I should be charmed—" began the cardinal; but Gozzi interposed in sincere alarm.

"For God's sake, Peter, do not encourage the rascal; the story will be an affair of hours, and we have much to accomplish before nightfall. Did you succeed in procuring a suitable gown for the girl, Jacques? You are accustomed to these matters; you have seduced several milliners, and your taste is impeccable."

"I have arranged for everything; I have ordered the supper, and bespoke the best string quartet in the four hospitals. The casino is in readiness; I have not yet relinquished its key to the new tenant, and my own servant has seen to it that there are fresh fires on the hearths, fresh candles in the girandoles, and fresh white roses in the crystal urns. I considered jasmine, I mused on lilies of the valley, but I knew I was wrong; there must be only white roses for this wedding-night. Am I not wise, your Eminence?"

Peter Innocent was at a loss to reply; his blue eyes were clouded by fatigue and bewilderment.

"Wedding-night?" he faltered, suddenly afraid. "Is it Virginio's wedding-night?"

"That is for your Eminence to say," the chevalier replied with courtly mendacity. "Also, it were only proper to await Virginio's own decision as to this momentous business; having seen Rosalba, I cannot question its affirmative nature. Carlo Gozzi and I have been planning a little surprise for the young people; a fête, *un petit diner à deux*, quite simple, you comprehend, but complete in every detail. It is Rosalba's birthday; since the noble Angelo Querini adopted her, her garments have been fashioned with a severe disregard of the prevailing *mode*, and frivolity has been absent from her life. Even at her coronation she was permitted no greater magnificence than a Greek robe of virgin white; the material was velvet, I believe, but the cut was antiquated. The Arcadian Academy has adored her manner of dressing, so chaste, so austere, so truly classical; but Rosalba has been unhappy. 'This was well enough for Ferney,' she has said, 'but for Venice, no! I can be young only once; am I never to have a single little stitch *alla francese*, not even a plain lemon-coloured Milordino with cloth of silver incisions, or a modest mantle of gold-green camelot lined with Canadian marten? I love my guardian with profound devotion, but I am, after all, a woman, and it is sad not to possess a robe of Holland *poussé*, trimmed with Spanish point!' Oh, she has wept, your Eminence; she has grieved in secret; we must endeavour to console her. What do you think; are you for flame or peach or girlish primrose? I am convinced it must be yellow. Tell me, do you agree?"

Around the cardinal's frosty and abstracted head a dozen rainbows seemed revolving in vertiginous arcs: colours of sun, of harvest moon, of comet's tail and hell-fire streamed out upon the increasing violet of dusk, and lit all Venice with their fervency. He hesitated, and Gozzi answered for him.

"That is a problem for you and the milliner's apprentice to determine ecstatically between yourselves; it does not concern Cardinal Bon. Peter, we have indeed hoped that our little festival in honour of these children might result in a wedding; for me there must ever be the happy conclusion to my fairy-tales, and I think to-night's performance will be the ultimate fantasy which I shall prepare for any stage. I do not care for the girl save as the inevitable partner for the prince; it is sufficient that she is pretty and not too intolerably a fool. But for Virginio I desire happiness, and over and above that good measure, a little pleasure running down, like shining bubbles, like golden grains. I had thought, myself, that what with music and dancing and a small quantity of very light wine to enliven them, the babes might frolic until dawn, and then we could all hire a gondola—for mine is at the pawnbroker's—and, proceeding to the church of Saint John and Saint Paul, allow Peter to pronounce the blessing of holy church upon their union. Then, perhaps, another gondola, and an *al fresco* breakfast upon the sands of the sea or in some rustic grove. What do you say, Peter?"

This time Peter Innocent was at the trembling point of reply, but the chevalier sent him back into silence by an ejaculation of surprise.

"Good heavens! What an insanity is this, my dear Count! Surely the marriage must take place before supper; it is only right and *convenable* if the young people are to dance together all night. I could never countenance such indiscretion; I am sincerely shocked. 'Frolic until dawn' indeed! But of course his Eminence will not permit it even for a moment."

"Confound you!" cried Carlo Gozzi. "You know perfectly well, Jacques, that I did not mean—"

"What?" said the chevalier, demurely.

The count looked at the cardinal; then he sighed deeply, and returned to its decaying sheath the jewelled Florentine dagger which his hand had for a moment caressed.

"Never mind; nothing. I meant nothing, since Peter Innocent is here; but beware how you annoy me, Chastelneuf."

"Oh, I intended no harm!" the chevalier assured him gaily. "I am possibly a trifle over-scrupulous about the conventions, but you must contrive to forgive a finical old friend, Carlo. We must all be very kind to-night; as for the marriage, I leave its hour to the choice of Cardinal Bon, and its subsequent good fortune to the benevolence of Almighty God." Casting a triumphant glance at Carlo Gozzi, Chastelneuf bowed his head in double humility to higher powers.

"If Virginio must really be married, I do not think it matters very much whether I marry him before or after supper," said Peter Innocent, gently. His delicately chiselled face was worn by anxiety, but his voice was firm as he continued: "I had hoped, as Carlo understands, that my dear nephew might find a conclusive felicity in the charitable embrace of the church, as I have done. My earthly joy has so nearly approached the heavenly, I have so thirsted for the peace of God and have been so thankfully appeased, that I had prayed for him a like simplicity of rapture. But if Carlo here, who has seen much of the lad's expanding soul, concludes that the complications of the secular life are indispensable to his content, so be it. Further, if the chevalier's account of young Rosalba Berni is but half so veracious as his proven honour must guarantee, I am well satisfied of her worthiness to be Virginio's wife. Therefore I will not withhold my consent from these nuptials; my heart awaits the lovers. Only, since it is better to avoid a too precipitate deed, however valid, let us follow Carlo's advice; the wedding shall take place to-morrow morning at the Church of Saint John and Saint Paul, whose benisons be upon these children."

The tower room was trembling in the violet dusk, like an island pinnacle invaded by the tide; the tide was evening, which rose rather than descended, flowing softly, smoothly, and invincibly from the deep lagoons, without the lightest undulation of a wave, without a sound, yet influential as the sea itself. Blue-violet and grey, red-violet where the sun informed it, the evening drowned the room in tinted darkness, until the faces of the three friends floated like nebulous ocean monsters in the gloom: Peter Innocent's face was coloured like a dead pearl, Carlo Gozzi's gleamed phosphorescent yellow. The chevalier's nervous hands wavered, brown as water weeds; his countenance was obscured.

The stairs which mounted to the tower chamber were crumbled and hazardous, yet upon their peril some one climbed, a footfall tinkled suddenly, incredibly tiny, a scampering as of winged mice, a skimming as of swallows. The rumour neared; heels or hoofs clicked upon stone at a fawn's pace; feathers or gauzy fabrics rustled and flew. The rusty latch cried out, the leathern door creaked in a draft, and Rosalba was within the room.

By some perverse vagary of the evening clouds, the sun and moon crossed swords above her head; under this pointed arch of light she ran into the room. The sun's long final ray was rosy and dim; the moon's first ray was silvery green and poignant. But Rosalba was pure gold from head to foot; she was brighter than the swords of light. A chaplet of golden leaves confined the burnished shadow of her hair; her sandal thongs were gilded; her gown, an Arcadian travesty of Diana's, was cut from cloth of gold. Her face was clear and pale, and her little freckles powdered it tenderly, like grains of golden dust. Her eyes were gold made magically translucent.

Her quick glance swept the apartment in a single scintillation, then, uttering a wild and joyous cry, she rushed upon Peter Innocent with all the ardour and velocity of a shooting star.

He was afraid. She was throttling him with her slender arms, and yet her lips were soft upon his cheek, and somewhere, in the profoundest caverns of his heart, love moved and wondered, answering her from a dream.

"Darling, even if you are a cardinal!" she said, "and lovely, even if you are an Eminence! Oh, you are beautiful, and like Virginio; I knew you at once! I shall adore you, and obey you always!" And she fell to kissing his hand. The fragility of those unresponsive and chilly finger-tips struck lightly yet insistently at her happiness, and she drew back in alarm, crying sadly:

"Oh, but you too, you too! You shiver and break when I touch you! Are you made of ice, that you cannot bear the little weight of my hand?"

Carlo Gozzi, to his own amazement, made a small sound of pity; the chevalier stepped forward and took the girl's hand between his own. He kissed it gravely and essayed to speak. At that precise instant the door swung open, and Virginio, sheathed in a silver cloak, came softly into the room; he entered like the twilight, and Rosalba was quenched within his arms.

XVIII: Too Many Pastry Cooks

"Inevitably ruin the meringue, as they say in Vienna!" the chevalier concluded lightly, closing his tortoise-shell snuff-box with a sharp click.

"Ah, you are right; the whole affair is whipped cream, and we are endeavouring to turn it into good solid butter." Carlo Gozzi agreed; his face was thoughtful and surprisingly humane upon the reflection. "What is man? A fantastical puff-paste, as Webster truly remarks."

"I implore you not to be forever quoting the English tragedians, my dear Count; it is disconcerting, to say the least, in this enlightened eighteenth century of ours. If Shakspere and his barbaric kin could have been gently licked into shape by the suave cat-tongue of Addison, they might have been endurable. As it is, I beg you to consider my earache, which is troublesome in November, and cannot brook a Gothic brutality of syllables. Touching the puff-paste, the simile is just enough, if Virginio is a man. I thought, however, we had determined him an elemental."

"H'm," said Gozzi, drily, "quite so, quite so. But, to my romantic fancy, an elemental moved among thunderstorms and whirlwinds; its least conceivable spirit was a snowfall. But Virginio is animated by the soul of an icicle or a small, pale skeleton leaf. I have no patience with him since he carries his arm in a sling."

"Come, come, my friend," cried Chastelneuf, "you are too hard on the boy. Rosalba is, after all, very impulsive; her dancing is hoydenish, and she is addicted to running races, like Atalanta gone mad. Look, there she is, at the end of the cypress alley; she seems to be indulging in a game of tag with his Eminence."

The scene, precisely etched in slender lines upon a clear green west of early winter, was the garden of a small casino near Venice; the hour was sunset. A delicate chill flavoured the atmosphere with a perfume of frost and fallen leaves; the chevalier wore his fur pelisse, and the count was wrapped in a Bedouin cape of camels' hair; his head was covered by a scarlet nightcap.

Over the lawn, powdered with blown yellow petals, the noble Angelo Querini approached; his grave and judicial garments reproved the perished flowers. He seated himself upon a marble bench by the side of the two friends, first spreading a shawl of Scottish plaid against the frigidity of the stone. His eyes sought the distant figure of Rosalba, which flitted unquietly along the vistas of the garden, exquisitely strange and savage in a cloak of tawny velvet lined with foxes' skins.

"She used never to be so wild a creature while she shared my roof," he said sadly. "She was always so studious, so docile, so domestic! God knows what possesses her poor little body; her tranquillity is turned to quicksilver. She runs like a rabbit, like a deer, to and fro within the confines of these walls, and at night she is very tired. I think she cries. She is afraid of Virginio."

"But Virginio is afraid of her!" cried Carlo Gozzi, rather angrily. "Rosalba is not afraid; she is a brave child. The boy is afraid; look at him now, leaning against the wall, as white as pumiced parchment, and as limp. He is a coward; how can he be afraid of a little woodland fawn like our Rosalba?"

It was true; the slim form of Virginio appeared crucified upon one of the stucco walls of the inclosure. His feet were crossed; his fair head drooped and fainted; one arm was outspread among the vines; the other hung in a black silk sling. There was an agony of weakness in the attitude; his transparent hand was clenched upon a broken tendril of vine.

"She is afraid of Virginio," Angelo Querini repeated obstinately.

"I believe you are both of you right; they are afraid of each other," said Chastelneuf. "Our experiment has not been wholly successful: two mild substances are, in the intimate fusion of marriage, beginning to effervesce; there are signs of an explosion. It is a pity, but the case is by no means hopeless."

Both Querini and Carlo Gozzi continued to stare indignantly at the pathetic spectacle of Virginio's despair. Querini felt a truly paternal solicitude for Rosalba, and Gozzi, upon learning that the girl was a confirmed admirer of his fairy drama, had quickly altered his opinion of her character and intellect. She appeared to him now the very embodiment of inner grace, and he reflected angrily that Virginio was a poor atomy to mate with this burning and spiritual child of love, who wore a wild beast's pelt above a heart more vulnerable than a little lamb's.

"The incident of the broken arm," drawled the chevalier, himself regarding Virginio through half-shut eyelids, "was, you comprehend, somewhat alarming to our young friend here. He is timid and fears to repeat the experience; his wife is impetuous and inclined to be careless. It is true that she did not actually touch him; they were running along the laurel alley, and he stumbled and fell. I was able to repair the damage, but it has shaken him seriously. Apparently he blames Rosalba; she, for her part, is proud, and in the consciousness of innocence, wounded to the soul by his implicit reproach. Neither will speak; their silence is like a darkness over them, in which suspicion flourishes."

"What does Peter say?"

"Nothing, in words; evidently he grieves, however, and I think he holds us responsible for the failure of his nephew's happiness. He feels certain that a monastery, rather than marriage is Virginio's natural haven. Rosalba he has forgiven, but he cannot look upon her without pain."

"Forgiven her! And for what fault, may I ask? Is it a crime on this unlucky infant's part that we have incontinently wedded her to a glass mannikin instead of decent blood and bone? God pardon us for our unholy meddling, for we have hurt the loveliest thing alive!"

Marvellous to relate, along the ancient leather of Carlo Gozzi's cheek a single glabrous tear moved slowly downward; the others observed it with awe, not attempting to answer until he had removed it with the sleeve of his burnous. Then the chevalier cleared his throat and spoke briskly.

"I share your indignation, my dear Count, but the fact remains. Peter has forgiven Rosalba; you know we cannot prevent Peter from forgiving people even when they have done no harm. He is incapable of harbouring resentment, but he must have the comfort of an occasional absolution to uphold him; he has remitted Rosalba's non-existent sins against Virginio. See how tenderly he addresses the elusive child. She shrinks, she starts like a doe transfixed by an arrow, yet Peter's shaft was feathered by compassion; he let fly from the strings of his heart. He is a saint whose silver niche should never know these invasive anxieties; I have erred in giving him a nephew."

Virginio stirred and wavered against the wall; languidly he straightened his slight limbs to glide across the grass toward his wife. He was very pale, and his beautiful face appeared mute, and blinded by mysterious sorrow; its smooth, pure contours were immobile as a mask of gauze over the countenance of one lately dead.

XIX: Burning Leaf

"It is a pity Rosalba is late; she is always so fond of *perdrix au choux*, and François has surpassed himself this evening," Chastelneuf commented reflectively, emptying his champagne goblet for the twelfth time.

The salon of the little casino was brilliantly, yet softly, illuminated by innumerable candles, and the Murano mirrors which formed its walls steeped the repeated lights in cool sea-coloured distances. The pyramid of grapes upon the table seemed moulded from the same silvered glass, and the flowers themselves were a fountain of crystalline spray. Peter Innocent, Carlo Gozzi, and Angelo Querini stained the pale, bright chamber with their black and rusty-brown attire; the chevalier's crimson startled it like a blow; only Virginio, resigned and pallid in pearly satin, fitted into the setting like a clear jewel clasped by a ring. His air of fragility was heightened by a cold and fearful lucency upon his brow; he looked ill, refused all food, and drank nothing save iced soda-water. He did not speak, but occupied his visibly shaking hands in the manufacture of little bread pellets. These were not grimy, as are the bread pellets of ordinary mortals; they appeared to acquire an added whiteness from the touch of his delicate and listless fingers.

"I overheard her tell Lucietta to repair the grey and lemon lutestring for to-night; one of the silver tassels was amiss, I think. Without doubt, she intended to dine with us; her absence begins to be alarming." Chastelneuf frowned into his replenished wineglass.

"I will go search for her," cried Querini and Carlo Gozzi with simultaneous eagerness. Gozzi was already upon his feet; Querini was rising majestically from his carven chair. Peter Innocent said nothing; the silence of Virginio became appreciably more profound.

"Your pardon, gentlemen; I believe I am best fitted for this embassy." The chevalier's voice was authoritative, and he was at the door in three great strides. "There is a bonfire in the garden," he threw back over his shoulder, like an irrelevant glove, as he passed from the room. The challenge, if challenge it were, seemed flung directly into Virginio's bloodless and impassive face. The boy was whiter than white glass, more quiet than fallen snow; his long, fair eyelashes were lowered over his chill cerulean eyes.

Chastelneuf ran hastily from the lighted house into the obscurity of the dusk; behind him the windows made tall parallelograms of radiance, tinted by curtains of rainbow silk; in front a stranger colour tore the darkness into ribbons and flew upward in fringes of scarlet. "Merely the leaves, which the gardener is burning," the chevalier told himself in reassurance.

Nevertheless his buckled shoes leaped over the ground like the hoofs of a stallion, and he reached the end of the laurel alley three seconds in advance of Rosalba, who had danced into his vision on the instant, lighter, brighter, and more insensate than a burning leaf. Her cloak of fox skins opened into wings, the air upheld her, and she floated into the heart of the fire.

In another second she was safe; Chastelneuf stood over her on the smoking grass and stamped out the sparks with his buckled shoes; he knelt, and crushed between his sinewy hands the little ruffle of flame which scalloped the edges of her crumpled gown.

"Why were you so wicked, so cruelly wicked?" he cried. "Why did you not tell me that you wished to die? Do you understand that I am always here to give you whatever you want? Yes, even if it is death, I will give it to you; but sweetly flavoured and in a golden box. I will give you the death of these others if you desire it; I will give you life such as you have not imagined save in heaven.

"My child, my child, you have observed that I love you, but have you comprehended the quality of my love? It is such as you will never discover in the hollow veins of Virginio or among the noble ganglions of Querini's intellect; it is love, lust, passion, humility, and wonder; it is human, not divine, not animal, but the love of mortal for mortal; it is at your service. I love you; I have loved many times and in many fashions, but this love is all your own. Use it as you will; I have no expectation that you can return it in kind. I have done you an irreparable wrong; forgive me; I entreat your forgiveness, my darling. I believed that I loved Virginio, for he is the fair product of my ingenuity, but in attempting to provide him with those things needful to happiness I have sacrificed you, who are worth a million pale Virginios. You are the true child of my heart, and its ultimate affection; I will even love you with a father's love, if I may not love you with a lover's. I will subdue my spirit to your least command if you will promise me to live!"

The chevalier spoke with the most impassioned fervour, and Rosalba smiled among her tawny furs to see him so perturbed. In the midst of her own despair, she perceived nothing save cause for mirth in the agitation of one whom she had always regarded as a benevolent elderly gentleman, respectably conversant with the Italian classics and the court circulars of Europe.

Chastelneuf experienced a pang of extreme humiliation; he felt Rosalba's eyes, wild and acute as those of a trapped vixen, transfix his chestnut peruke and pierce to the silver stubble beneath it. The wrinkles upon his face were deepened as by acid, and his falcon look grew weary with the recollection of unrestful years. Rosalba, innocent alike of cruelty or compassion, shifted her gaze without speaking, and then cried aloud in the voice of a prisoned creature tardily released. Virginio, so veiled in twilight as to appear no more than a moving part of the invisible, now glided from the obscurity of the garden.

Rosalba shot upward like an impulsive flower nourished on subterranean flame; she ran, a pointed blossom of the dragon seed, straight to Virginio's heart. She might have been a dagger in that heart; the boy drew himself erect, closed his eyes, and stood swaying in an agony apparent as a wound. There was another and a sharper cry, an echo and a confused murmuring; the two slim figures clung together for an instant. Then they were again divided; the blue translucent dusk flowed between them like a narrow river; they stretched their hands to each other, and their tears fell into the swift and narrow stream of time and were lost.

Chastelneuf forgot his own sorrowful anger in a sudden pity; he was intolerably saddened by the spectacle of the lovers' frustration. He wanted nothing half so much as to see them happy and at peace under the evening stars; their youth was darling to his senses, like the smell of flowers or the flavour of wine, and he observed it without envy. He relinquished the luxury of self-commiseration, and reminding his vanity how easily he might have been Rosalba's parent, he cleared his throat, straightened his chestnut peruke, and spoke.

"My children," he said in a tone admirably paternal and concerned, "I am inexpressibly grieved to witness your distress; I am forced to conclude that all is not well between you. Trust me to understand your reticences, but trust me yet again, and further, to resolve your problems in my larger experience. If you will confide in me, my dears, I can convince you of my ability to assist you in any dilemma."

Even as he pronounced the words with such judicial calm, his mind was troubled and his bowels wrung by a dreadful premonition; pity grew fierce as anger in his soul, and his heart gnawed at his ribs.

Dimly as he now discerned the two figures confronting each other across the profound spaces, coloured more ambiguously than twilight, of their mutual and mortal fear, he was yet aware of a difference in air and attitude, which made Rosalba, to the peculiar pattern of his own mind, the sadder by an infinity of pain.

Virginio stood silent and curiously withdrawn; his white satin shoes were rooted to the ground, but he swayed in the windless atmosphere, and the rustle of his garments and the glimmer of his flaxen hair made a faint music and a fainter illumination, like the stir of a sapling birch tree in the dark.

"Virginio?" said Rosalba, softly.

The rustle of silk and the glimmer of silvery gold appeared, to the chevalier's watchfulness, to assume a new quality; the one had the tinkle, the other the sheen, of something cold and glassy. The sapling birch tree wore no leaves; its slender branches were incased in crystal, and at the tip of every twig a smooth bright icicle hung tremulous.

"Virginio?" said Rosalba again, and again softly, but now she said it with despair.

The girl fluttered restlessly about; she was light as thistledown or dancing flame. Her little hands, emerging from the loose, voluminous wings of her mantle, were lifted continually towards Virginio in a gesture of supplication, mockery, and compassion. Although, in her brilliance, she was fire to Virginio's crackling ice, the chevalier remembered suddenly that the essential substance of that element is delicate and tender and more malleable than the very air, whereas ice is denser even than water, and often hard as stone. And he reflected truly that it was Rosalba's spirit that must inevitably be wounded in this unnatural warfare, however brittle Virginio's bones might prove.

"Have you no word to say to me, my children?" he entreated, and at last Rosalba answered him. She turned from Virginio with recovered composure, and faced Chastelneuf with a look of great dignity and sedateness.

"I shall be most grateful for your support and guidance, Chevalier," she said politely. All tint or tremor of the fantastic had fallen from her aspect, and she was nothing stranger than a slight, elegant girl in a velvet cloak, who strove to appear haughty despite her evident fatigue, and whose pale and pretty countenance was wet with ingenuous human tears.

XX: Spiderweb Tangle

"I am willing," cried Rosalba, "to do anything; anything, everything, or nothing; I am the servant of the chevalier's advice."

"Anything within reason," amended Querini; his ward interrupted him with quite unfilial scorn.

"Oh, but anything, within or without, or far from reason as the moon from sirocco or I from Notre Dame de Paris! Reason is for old gentlemen, like you and M. de Voltaire; the chevalier understands my determination."

Chastelneuf, thus suddenly made free of the dedicated insanity of youth, smiled into the fire of cedar logs, pervaded by a sweeter, more scented warmth than theirs.

"Reason is not the goddess of emergencies." Carlo Gozzi spoke sententiously, ruffling his thin hair above a corrugated brow. Peter Innocent said nothing.

The little apartment was charming with its fawn-coloured *boiseries* and rose-garlanded carpet; the books behind their gilded lattices enriched the walls by a soft and variegated pattern of their own. The room was called the *study*, after an English fashion; its air was warm and intimate. Every one, with the exception of Virginio, preferred it to the pale and mirrored salon where he now sat alone, nibbling a long green strip of angelica and idly perusing the pages of Frederick Martens' "Natural History of Spitzbergen." "There grows an Arctic flower," he read; but his tranquillity was now and again shattered by the heat and hurry of voices from the open door.

"It is the only solution," pronounced the chevalier. His passing glow was fled, and melancholy possessed him, hollowing his eyes and parching the accustomed glibness of his speech. "I had forgotten my youth, I think," he continued, subdued to shame. "I remembered love, for that still lives in my breast, but I did not remember the races which I ran with Caterina in the gardens of Saint Blaise; my rheumatisms obscured my mind. Virginio can embrace his wife in comfort; his body is attuned to marital bliss. I arranged for that; it was in my opinion of the first importance. But I totally neglected to provide for the lighter contingencies of courtship; he cannot support the rigours of hide-and-seek or the excitement of a bout of blindman's-buff. A handspring would be the end of him. He is a perfect husband, I assure you, but he can never be a playmate for this poor child. When you are older, my dear, it will not grieve you; the domestic pleasures of the *foyer* will suffice."

He ceased; Rosalba was weeping uncontrollably.

"No! no!" she murmured through her tears, "it is too difficult; I cannot bear it! Better a thousand times some violent change, some mad and excessive sacrifice! I lie in his arms at night; my breath is stilled because I love him, and his kisses close my lips over my laughter and my eyelids over my tears. But in the morning, when there is no more moonlight, and the sun is shining with the insistence of a golden trumpet made fire instead of sound, when all the red and yellow cockerels are crowing and the larks fly upward like particles of flame, then when I wake and look at him he is afraid. He trembles; when I spring up in the sunshine he trembles at my side; when I run to the window, he pulls the covers about his ears; when I fling the curtains apart to let the light rush in, he faints upon his pillow; the delicate vibration of the dawn afflicts him like a thunderstroke. I tell you, it is too difficult; I cannot bear it, and I would rather die than have it so."

"This is intolerably sad," said Peter Innocent. "The girl is not to blame, yet perhaps we shall have to put her into a convent."

But, "Never! never! never!" cried his three companions with an equal rage, and Rosalba fell upon her knees before him and anointed his hands with her despair.

"There is nothing for it, after all, but the magic," the chevalier repeated solemnly. With the utmost gentleness he raised Rosalba to her feet and conducted her to the shelter of a winged armchair near the hearth.

Reflected firelight rose and fell in rays upon her face, so that it shone unquietly between golden pallor and the colour of blushes; so also her ringlets were transformed from bright to dark and back again to brighter. The gauzes of her dress were disarranged, and among their folds hung here a pink and here a scarlet leaf, and here a frosty flake of ashes. Always she seemed to move and waver in the leaping light, stirred partly by its changes and partly by the shaking of her own heart, and although she was slight and shaken, her look was brave and vibrant and alive.

"Yes, the magic by all means," she said

eagerly, quickened to fervour by a radiance above and beyond the cedar flames. "I am not afraid; it will not hurt me if I am not afraid."

"Non dolet!" cried Angelo Querini in a terrible voice, shielding his countenance from view.

"But you can assure us that it will be purely beneficent, or white magic, my dear friend?" asked Peter Innocent, with anxious concern; he was shocked by the violence of the chevalier's reply.

"I can assure you of nothing so absurd, your Eminence. The Deity may justly approve of the affair of Virginio; He cannot seriously object to the vivification of a few handfuls of harmless Murano sand and a pipkin of holy water. But it is another and a very different matter to deprive one of His creatures of the delights and powers bestowed upon her by Himself; we shall require the devil's aid in murdering Rosalba."

"Murder? Surely we are not talking of murder!" Peter Innocent made the sign of the cross, shivering visibly in the blast of horror invoked by the loud and bloody word.

"Ah, not officially, perhaps." The chevalier's bitterness was profound and quiet; absently he lifted Rosalba's warm, sunburnt little hand to his twisted lips.

"We shall, indeed, leave her the privilege of living; possibly, in her new and chastened state, she may be duly grateful. But of this Rosalba, this child who sits before us clothed in light and eloquent with the breath of God—of this Rosalba nothing will remain. Yet, if you prefer, we need not call it murder."

"Remember that it is my own wish; the cardinal would have sent me to a convent."

The girl spoke gently and without irony, but Chastelneuf bowed his head as if a millstone hung upon his breast; what depth of water closed above that head, or whether tinged with salt or vinegar or gall, it were worse than useless to conjecture.

"It is your own wish; I will not dispute it," he said humbly. "I am, in point of fact, responsible for the plan; I myself proposed it, and, indeed, it appears to be the only unravelling, save the convent, of this deplorable tangle. Of course I could always rescue you from the convent," he added hopefully and under his breath to Rosalba. The girl did not heed him; her eyes were fixed upon Peter Innocent, and she addressed that venerable prelate with the desperate courage of a suppliant.

"I am no more afraid of black magic than of white, Eminence. In the whole world there is only one thing of which I am afraid, and that thing is Virginio's fear. Let me suffer this ordeal, whatever it may prove, and live thereafter in peace and contentment with my beloved husband; this is all I ask."

"A sacrifice proffered in such tenderness cannot come amiss to the mercy of God." Peter Innocent put forth his veined, transparent hand in a gesture of reassurance, and Rosalba thanked him with a pale, but valiant, smile.

"I shall have a word to interpose in this matter," said Angelo Querini. "I do not believe in magic, either black or white; it is not rational, logical, or decent. I do not wish Rosalba to be mixed up in necromancy and kindred follies."

"I believe in magic, and that so religiously that I cannot countenance such practices as the chevalier proposes; the danger to a simple child like Rosalba is appalling. It is well enough, when I write of it, for the negress Smeraldina to be dipped into a cauldron of flame, emerging whiter than a clay pipe, but for this little firebird to be caught and frozen into lifelessness, that is another story altogether, too tragic for my perusal. Let us turn her into a fawn or a vixen or a tawny panther, and set her free forever."

XXI: Method of the Brothers Dubois

"There is a villa at Strà, upon the banks of the Brenta, whose aviaries contain eagles from the Apennines, and whose fenced inclosures hold captive a hundred stags, wild roe, and mountain goats. Do you believe, because the hornbeam is green and the myrtle fragrant, that these creatures are happy? Rosalba, enchanted into some savage form, would wound her bosom against thorny walls, and find herself a prisoner among invisible labyrinths. She would still be bound fast to Virginio, to run like a hound at his heel, or flutter falconwise to his wrist. This were no freedom, but a strange refinement of pain. Rather let her shrink into a china doll and have done with feeling than that she should assume wings prematurely broken or a hind's fleetness without liberty of heart!"

"You are an orator, M. de Chastelneuf; allow me to congratulate you upon your eloquence." Thus spoke the noble Angelo Querini, one time senator of the Republic of Venice. "It might, however, be employed in some worthier cause than the wilful deception of a young girl. We have none of us forgotten Madame von Wulfe and the cruel farce of *Quérilinth*."

"I thank you for the compliment, my dear Querini; your approbation is ever welcome. For the insult I forgive you, even as I hope Madame von Wulfe has forgiven me. In the present matter I can have no motive other than altruism, and I assure you of my good faith. Nevertheless, it is for Rosalba to decide whether or no I now embark upon what must prove for all concerned a solemn and hazardous undertaking."

"I wish it; I demand it," Rosalba answered firmly. "Desperate as the means must be, it is my only remedy for torment. I am prepared to incur the equivalent of death in order to achieve peace for Virginio."

"The child is one of God's elected angels!" cried Peter Innocent in awe. "If she should unhappily perish in this dark adventure, she must in common fairness be canonized. Meanwhile I wish I had her safe among the Poor Clares of Assisi; she is too saintly for this secular arena of mortal life."

"Nonsense! She is nothing of the sort;

she is merely a luckless girl who loves a glass manikin instead of kind, consoling flesh and blood!" the chevalier retorted with sardonic insolence. It was plain that his own flesh and blood were racked and poisoned by revolt.

M. de Chastelneuf was very pale. His eyes were sunken in his head, and his face was ravaged like a starving man's. Yet, worn and sharpened and intolerably wrung, he still maintained, despite this betrayal of his body, a certain victory of spirit, a simple affair of courage, perhaps, and accustomed coolness against heavy odds. And again, it was plain that he did not suffer for himself alone.

"Above all, we must be practical," he said, recovering perfectly his manner of impudent composure. "There is a method—not my own, I may say, but that of the celebrated Brothers Dubois, late of Vincennes—whereby young ladies are rendered harmless to the tranquillity of others and permanently deprived of their surplus emotions. Quite frankly, it is magic of a vehement and painful variety; the subject is ultimately transformed into fine porcelain, but the process is not agreeable, and the result, although miraculous, is somewhat inhuman. I have known fathers who submitted their daughters to the ordeal, husbands who forced it upon their wives, but never, until this hour, have I known a woman to desire the torture of her own free will. It is an agony more incisive than birth or dissolution; I dare not veil the circumstance with pity."

"And may a woman undergo this terrible ordeal and live?" Carlo Gozzi alone found voice, and that the thinnest whisper, to inquire.

"Yes, she may live, and flourish, and be fair and decorous and delightful." Chastelneuf ground his strong white teeth upon the words. "She may, to all appearances and outward seeming, remain a mortal woman; for aught I know to the contrary a purified soul may burn peacefully within the pretty fabric of her body. But—she will be porcelain; fine porcelain, remember, and no longer clay. In a porcelain vessel filled with clear water a rose may live for a little while, but out of clay a rose may rise alive and blooming, set on the roots of elder roses. There is a difference, but it does not matter."

"Nothing matters except Virginio," said Rosalba, softly.

Even as the chevalier drove sharp nails into his palms and bit his lip until he tasted blood, even as Peter Innocent bowed his lovely silver brow in sorrowful acquiescence, Virginio entered quietly and sadly, like the softer echo of Rosalba's voice.

None who looked upon him then wondered afterward at the fabulous chivalry of the girl's devotion; the lovers looked into each other's eyes, and their eyes were tender, pitiful, and afraid. Virginio wore a quality of pure translucent beauty, unwarmed by earth, the beauty of an element like sea or air, or that refined and rarefied sunlight mirrored by the moon. He wore this beauty meekly, and with a slight and delicate timidity he approached his wife and folded her within his arms. Felicity hovered above their bending heads, flying nearer, yet never alighting; the wings of felicity were so nearly visible that to Carlo Gozzi they appeared feathered like those of the pigeons of Saint Mark, and to Peter Innocent like the Holy Ghost itself in the shape of a silver dove.

Furthermore, to Peter Innocent, whose mind was a missal book of sacred images, Virginio figured as the young John Baptist, wandering immaculate in the desert, and Rosalba as a small golden lioness, of equal virtue and simplicity, but pagan and untamable and shy.

So, like a pair of legendary children, they

came to the cardinal where he sat musing by the fire, and, moved by one impulse, sank upon their knees before him and inclined their bright locks to his blessing. The flaxen and the darkly burnished head bent side by side beneath his hand, and Peter Innocent's musings were made audible as prayer, and in the silence smoke rose like incense from the crumbling cedar logs, ascending through the chimney to the frosty night, and thence perhaps, to heaven.

XXII: Pâte Tendre

"If you were hard paste, we should have to send you to Meissen," said the chevalier, smiling and alert in an elegant new travelling-cloak of bottle-green broadcloth. The midday sun lay yellow along a vast map spread upon the writing-desk, and although it was November, the windows stood open to sweet and jocund breezes. An atmosphere of nervous gaiety pervaded the study; a strapped portmanteau and a Florentine dressing-case occupied the settee, and seven large bandboxes were piled in a corner.

Upon the mantelpiece two crystal vases exhaled a mist of jasmine, and between these were set a number of china figurines of exquisite workmanship. A fantastic bellarmine grimaced at a Bow cupid, and a delicious Chelsea group of the Four Seasons, modelled by Roubiliac, and glowing with every floral tint, contrasted curiously with a fine white Derby biscuit statuette of Queen Charlotte and her children.

"Yes, Meissen for hard paste," repeated Chastelneuf, cheerfully, "and from that grim fortress you might come forth with a rosy Saxon complexion and no sensibilities whatever."

"And no freckles?" asked Rosalba, with a pardonable feminine eagerness.

"No, my love; you would be as pink as a sugar-plum and as smooth as whipped cream. However, Meissen is far too Germanic for your peculiar mentality, and you could never survive its furnaces. It must be either Sèvres or Marseilles, since Hannong of Strasburg has been dead these two years, and you are averse to visiting England."

"I cannot forget that I am a Frenchwoman." Rosalba spoke with a faint trace of hauteur, gazing rather wistfully at the Chelsea figure of Spring, attired in a vernal dress of apple green and pearl colour.

"I should like to see you in white Marseilles faïence," said the chevalier. "I once beheld a shepherdess in biscuit-porcelain, made in the factory of the Duc de Villeroy at Mennecy, which was almost worthy of you. Nevertheless, I believe we shall be wise in selecting Sèvres. It was the scene of the Brothers Dubois's amazing discovery; they were subsequently dismissed for drunkenness and the practice of venomous magic. They came to me with letters from the Prince of Courland, whom they had greatly assisted in the search for the philosopher's stone. I was able to resolve the slight difficulties they had encountered by means of my infallible compound of Hungarian crystal and native cinnabar. Overcome with gratitude, they presented me with the secret recipe associated with their name. Since then I have ever been in a position to turn ladies into porcelain, but I have not often availed myself of the opportunity; the process is opposed to my principles and natural proclivities."

"Dear Chevalier, I am quite familiar with your sentiments," murmured Rosalba, sympathetically and a little shyly. "But you will surely not refuse to aid me, upon this occasion, in my search for happiness. I have understood you to say, have I not, that you are capable of complete and single-handed success in the absence of the Brothers Dubois?"

"But yes, and fortunately, since the Brothers Dubois are at present inaccessibly situated in purgatory or some even less salubrious region," Chastelneuf assured her. "I need no help in the matter, save that of such skilled workmen as are to be found in any porcelain factory, augmented by those supernatural agencies which I must not scruple to employ."

"I am glad it is to be Sèvres, when all is said and done." Rosalba gazed reflectively into a tortoise-shell mirror, comparing her image therein with the countenance of an enchanting china figure, sculptured by Clodion in the classic taste, which the chevalier, bowing, presented to her view, poised daintily upon the palm of his hand.

"Oh, it is undoubtedly your *genre!*" cried Chastelneuf with enthusiasm, touching the girl's pale cheek with a respectfully tentative forefinger. "The true Sèvres, the soft paste of the old régime, not this stony stuff they have derived from the Germans. You are the finest *porcelaine de France;* I know the ingredients." And he began to chant a medley of words, in which Rosalba was at some pains to distinguish syllables analogous to "Fontainebleau sand—pure sea salt—Aliante alum—and powdered alabaster." Certainly the chevalier was a gentleman of various and esoteric learning, whose knowledge of humanity was both profound and nice. Rosalba resigned her will to his, and faced the future with mingled fortitude and acute curiosity.

"It is decided, then, that the cardinal accompany us, while Virginio remains with Querini and Carlo Gozzi, perfecting himself in the study of Greek, Latin, Arabic, and antique Spanish. He will thus be enabled to compare philosophies with fairy-tales, and to contemplate life with the stoicism of the one and the insouciance of the other. I have also suggested that he become proficient upon the flute and engage a really good fencing-master," said the chevalier, divesting himself of his travelling cloak and taking a pinch of snuff.

"We depart in an hour's time," he continued lightly, consulting a sumptuous jewelled watch, "and you will doubtless prefer to make your adieus to Virginio unattended by the most affectionate friend. I withdraw, therefore, but shall await you, with restrained impatience, in the adjoining apartment. I am sure we shall have no cause to regret our decision in the matter of factories." His smile contrived a positive frivolity, and Rosalba experienced a thrill of gratitude.

"The cardinal makes me feel that I am setting forth upon a penitential pilgrimage," she said plaintively. "You are less alarming; allow it to remain a mere affair of millinery. I could almost believe that we were going to Paris to select a costume for the carnival."

"But that, in a way, is true enough, my child," cried Chastelneuf, retiring. As he went, he coughed thrice behind a fine lace handkerchief, and wiped his eyes.

Presently Virginio knocked gently upon the door, and entered like a cloud of cooler air.

"Adieu, Virginio, my darling," whispered Rosalba.

"Adieu, adieu, my heart's beloved," the boy replied. Their voices were too low for audible trembling, but their hands, clinging together in the final instant, shook like thin white petals in a hurricane.

"Virginio, good-bye."

"Good-bye, Rosalba."

"I am going."

"I know; good-bye, my love."

"Virginio—"

"My dear—"

"Good-bye."

They embraced; bright glassy tears fell upon Rosalba's breast, and upon Virginio's cold hands Rosalba's tears fell quick and glittering as sunshower drops, and warm almost as the kisses wherewith they were mingled.

The great door closed at last between the lovers, leaving no sound; its painted panels confronted them severally with Pan's cruel nonchalance and Medusa's uncomfortable stare.

Virginio examined his finger-nails; they were quite uninjured, but the least finger of his left hand appeared to have suffered a slight sprain.

Rosalba, drawing on her white suède gloves, observed without surprise that both her wrists were faintly flecked with blood, as though a bracelet of thorns had lately clasped them.

XXIII: Ordeal by Fire

Through a landscape lightly strewn with snow, and rendered graciously austere by long, converging lines of leafless poplars, the three strange travellers approached the neighbourhood of Paris.

The chevalier's English carriage was commodious and softly cushioned, and the discomforts of the journey had been negligible; nevertheless a ponderable sadness was bound upon the shoulders of the adventurers, as if indeed they carried ambiguous packs too heavy for their spirits. Their chins were sunk against their breasts, and even Chastelneuf strove quite in vain to dissipate this burden by companionable chatter.

"Paris must wait," he observed to Rosalba. "Afterward, when our affair is concluded, it will be time to think of the *trousseau*, which only Paris can fitly provide for a Frenchwoman. I consider you too fine for our Venetian barbarities of fashion, which tend ever to the extravagant and the capricious. You must see Bertin, of course; the queen swears by her, although the little

Polignac, always so demure and so chic, is of another opinion entirely. But you will choose for yourself; it is the prerogative of Venus."

Rosalba raised her satirically penciled brows the least reproving shade, and the chevalier subsided into a conversation with Peter Innocent, who remained immersed in his breviary, vouchsafing now and again an absent-minded nod or a grieved monosyllable in response to the other's volubility.

"While I warmly second your decision as to the preservation of the strictest incognito, Eminence, I can assure you that no such peril attaches itself to our activities in this enlightened land of France as we should inevitably incur at home. In Venice we should have the Holy Office upon our tracks in a twinkling; here we need only fear the unfriendly attention of the Academy of Sciences.

"Instead of the Three and their spies, we must shun the associates of Bailly and Franklin. They are about to disturb the magnetic afflatus of Mesmer, but he, you know, is a charlatan."

"Yes?" said Peter Innocent, clutching his rosary.

They drove through the Forest of Meudon; beyond lay the park and the two châteaux. The sun was setting somewhere over their left shoulders.

"Have you heard that the duc de Chartres is cutting down the magnificent chestnut alleys in the Palais-Royal?" inquired the chevalier.

His companions preserved a silence unbroken save by sighs.

Presently they reached the outskirts of the ancient town of Sèvres; at a little distance from the factory, whose dark bulk rose upon the river-bank, a curious tower was conspicuous above a clump of nameless trees.

"Private workroom of the Brothers Dubois," the chevalier explained in hushed, oppressive accents.

"But they are dead, and the place is evidently deserted!" cried the cardinal, his voice vibrating to the chill along his spine.

"True; only too true," said Chastelneuf.

Perhaps the vitreous tiles which roofed the structure possessed a coppery glaze, perhaps the doors and windows were bound with this red metal, or perhaps the setting sun performed a sinister miracle of transmutation, and turned the tower into blood and flame. Its shape was very singular and menacing against the holy evening sky, where upon a field of violet a few small stars were visible. The carriage halted at a word from Chastelneuf, and came to a standstill at the mouth of a clearing in the clump of trees; feathery grasses, tipped with snow, had overgrown the path. The horses stamped their feet in the stillness; steam floated in thick clouds about their heads. The chevalier's Spanish servant, shrouded to the eyes in a sombre cloak, awaited his master's instructions with an air of taciturn complicity in some questionable design.

"Monseigneur, you will proceed to the inn at Versailles, where a fire, a feather bed, and a roasted fowl are in readiness," Chastelneuf declared, fixing the cardinal with an hypnotic eye. "Rosalba and I must now go on alone."

"On foot?" Peter Innocent asked in a weak voice.

"On foot, but not far; Rosalba will have ample opportunity to dry her slippers before the night is out." The words were significant and sharp; the cardinal shuddered.

"I am not afraid," said Rosalba, for the thousandth time, in a pitiful whisper. "They do not throw salt into the furnaces any more, nor use pulverized ox-bones, as they do in England."

"She need not suffer a second firing," said Chastelneuf. "I have concluded that no glaze is necessary, though, for that matter, the modern glaze is no longer by immersion, but by sprinkling, as in Christian baptism. But we shall leave Rosalba in the simple biscuit state. Console yourself, Eminence; your responsibility is heavy, but she shall be saved."

Peter Innocent found a slight support for his swooning spirit in the religious flavour of these final reassurances; he watched the pair depart through tears, and made his every breath a prayer as the trees met over the chevalier's haughty head and took Rosalba into their equivocal embrace.

For one brief instant the tower was split by a streak of brightness, and all the vehemence of fire outraged the tranquillity of the twilit wood; then the door closed, the smoke dispersed, the fumes faded in air, and with their going Peter Innocent was borne like thistledown, by the swift agency of two black horses, along the lonely road to Versailles.

XXIV: Silver Cord

In the ancient Satory quarter of Versailles, under the very shadow of the new cathedral of St. Louis, there lay a little tavern whose sign bore the symbol of the Silver Bowman. In the only parlour the narrow place afforded a clear fire had been kindled, before whose consolatory incandescence the Cardinal Peter Innocent Bon now warmed his hands and meditated upon the wonders of the world.

The eighth of these, to his enchanted thinking, and which had but this moment vanished in a visible smoke from between his fingers, was not the greater nor the smaller Trianon, nor yet the palace itself, nor the gardens nor the orangery. The thing had been more marvellous than these, both magic and geometric; a flower inclosed in a carven frame, a lovely formal pattern. A flake of snow, fallen from the dove-coloured skies of France, had melted in the heat of the fire.

Although Peter Innocent had often found the Roman winter of a severity too poignant for his anatomy to support without pain, he had rarely encountered the mysteries of frost and snow, and now his recollection wandered to the Christmas season of 1716, when he had seen Venice no longer blue and gold, but muffled and masked in whiteness. Oblivion like sleep had come at first upon the town, and then a bitter wind, and finally, when the sun shone again in the heavens, the palaces and church towers had flashed and scintillated beneath a covering of quicksilver. All this was memorable to Peter Innocent after many years, and he could picture the wine shop, even, where his father had taken him for a glass of malvasia from Epirus. He had been fourteen years old at the time, the malvasia had tasted warm as imagined Acroceraunian spring.

Since then, and so for uncounted Christmas seasons, Peter Innocent had forgotten the miracle of snow. Now he was enraptured, and opening the casement against a stubborn blast of the north, he filled his hands once more with the intricate crystals.

Yet all too soon the crystals dissolved again to icy moisture, and Peter Innocent considered beauty's evanescence as typified in those spilt drops of snow water.

A thin white wine of France stood in a green decanter by his elbow, but he foretasted it as cold astringent stuff; he wished

Rosalba would return to brew him a glass of negus, with nutmeg in it, and the grated rind of a lemon.

A small volume bound in creamy vellum lay by the decanter, in a pool of green reflected light; he knew it for a copy of Rosalba's poems, printed at Pisa less than a year ago as a gift from Querini to his ward.

An absurd medley of quotation sprinkled the title-page with tags from Seneca and Catullus. Here cried the unchristian wastrel to his strumpet: "Remains to be slept the sleep of one unbroken night." Here the virtuous philosopher remarked, with equal gloom: "We are kindled and put out." Peter Innocent found the poems themselves hard to decipher in the failing light.

He picked up a fine Venetian edition of Theocritus, but the book fell open at an unknown line, and this is what he read: "The lamb is gone, the poor young thing is gone . . . a savage wolf has crunched her in his jaws, and the dogs bay; what profits it to weep, when of that lost creature not a bone nor a cinder is left?"

Peter Innocent poured out a measure of the thin white wine; the goblet was full to the brim, and a little wine was spilled upon the pages of the book, for the cardinal's hand was trembling. He shivered, huddled in his worn habit of the Friars Minor; he wished very heartily that he had indeed borrowed the chevalier's luxurious dressing-gown of quilted purple silk, as Rosalba had more than once suggested.

The streets of Versailles were veiled by falling snow, and the wheels of the few cabriolets and chariots which passed beneath the window of the inn were noiseless in their revolutions; only the occasional crack of a whip shattered the frosty silence. Peter Innocent was very lonely.

Almost, he believed, he would have welcomed the arrival of those visitors whom his shy secretiveness had so far avoided. His incognito had been studiously preserved; even the curious eye of Louis de Rohan Guéménée, Cardinal Grand Almoner and Archbishop of Strasburg, had failed to mark the elusive wearer of the grey-brown garb of St. Francis.

With the benediction of Assisi's name, there came into Peter Innocent's mind a sudden longing to be comforted, and he turned, like a bewildered child, to the dear protection of his patron saint. His fingers sought and found the leaves of another book, wherein his own scholarly Italian hand had traced certain passages from the life of Francis. His sight, under the encroaching dusk, grew dim; then he saw plainly what was written in the book.

"O brother fire, most beautiful of all creatures, be courteous to me at this hour, knowing how well I have always loved thee and ever will for His love Who created thee!"

Upon the instant, the fire upon the hearth appeared to lift its terrible head in anger and spring like a tiger at his throat; he put up his feeble arms in a defensive gesture, and dropped them again in despair. The portent was revenge from heaven.

For even now, at his advice, at his desire, Rosalba was giving her body to be burned. "Be courteous to me at this hour—" The hour was struck, and the jaws of the furnace had received the child.

He caught up the decanter of wine, and flung it, a bubble of green glass, into the burning fangs of the fire, where it was destroyed in a moment. Then he fell upon his knees, and would have beat out the flames with his hands; but his strength failed him, the monster leaped upward with a roar, and Peter Innocent felt its teeth fasten in his shoulder; then he fainted.

He was revived by the chevalier's voice and Rosalba's touch upon his temples. The window stood open to the snow, which blew inward, golden particles emerging strangely from an infinity of blue dusk; a handful of snow was sprinkled over his eyes, which throbbed with fever. The fire still raged within its bars, but as Rosalba stooped to tend it, he could have sworn that she spoke in a low, caressing tone, and perhaps admonished it by a sign; presently the flames sank down and seemed to slumber.

The chevalier's cloak was wet with snow, and his face confessed a weariness and lassitude most carefully excluded from his speech.

"All is well, Eminence," he said, flinging his laced hat upon the table with a long-drawn sigh of fatigue. "She has survived our ministrations; a diabolic ordeal has served its purpose, and she has returned to you alive. Of her courage I cannot speak; her present composure may speak for her, even in silence. Yet perhaps, of her charity, she has a word for those who have wronged her."

Rosalba leaned at ease against the window-frame, and the snow blew past her lifted head and powdered it with particles of gold. There was about her an air of perfect calm; she was poised, composed, and quiet, yet without stiffness; her attitude had the grace of a bird arrested in flight, a flower flexible, but unmoved by wind. Peter Innocent knew instinctively that her spirit was unstirred by any pang that may not be suffered by an exemplary child of seven.

Her face was exquisitely clear and fresh in every tilted line and smooth velvety surface; her hair was miraculously symmetrical, and its thick scallops had the quality of gilded bronze. Her mantle fell about her in delicate sculptured folds.

"God give you peace!" said Rosalba to Peter Innocent, with a gentle candour unaware of pity and its intolerable demands.

XXV: Interior by Longhi

How delicate a contrivance of language must lull the imagination to repose before it may sing or picture to itself, while half-asleep, Rosalba's homecoming!

This must be spoken in a whisper, dreamed in a meditation, drawn in the palest colours of pearls, set to an accompaniment of reverential music, veiling silence with a silver veil.

In that hour when the shadows flow like clear blue water along the golden sands of day, in the mildness of afternoon, in a place profoundly quiet, Virginio and Rosalba met and kissed.

Their very garments were awed into submission, so that silk dared not rustle or flowers shed their fragrance; the heels of their shoes were dipped in magic, so that they made no sound, and a dimness like the smoke of incense obscured the shining of their hair.

Nothing else in the world was ever so soft as their lips and the clasp of their hands; these were softer than the wings of grey moths or the frosty feathers of dandelion seed.

A little brush, smoothing thin pigments on a polished cedar panel, may trace more lightly and precisely than any pen the figures of Virginio and Rosalba, the wedded lovers of a fairy-tale, who now live happy ever after, in Venice, in a world of porcelain and Murano mirrors.

It has been said, and that upon distinguished authority, that Pietro Longhi survived, in the amber peace of a mellowing century, until the age of eighty; the statement is difficult to refute.

For those who would believe it, there exists in support of this theory a small painting, bearing the artist's signature not only in the mere syllables of his name, but, more convincingly, in every curve and colour of the scene itself.

The hand of a very old man is evident in the fine performance; the lines waver, the colours are subdued and etherealized. The hand is the hand of Longhi, and he was an old man when Rosalba returned to Venice in the amber twilight of a dying century.

This twilight fills the picture, and is reflected from the mirrors of the background; the faces of the lovers emerge like stars from this profundity of twilight. The figure of

Peter Innocent is there, quiet as a carven saint in his niche; he wears the grey-brown habit of the Friars Minor, and his veined and fragile hands are folded upon a cross. That noble brow and faint ironic smile can only be Querini's, and Count Carlo Gozzi looks impish and melancholy in a new periwig and the rich mantle of a patrician. The chevalier is absent; it is said he has retired to Bohemia.

The faces of the lovers are most beautiful and pure; the gentle and elegiac quality of their love appears unmarred by longing. Having forgotten fear and the requirements of pity, their tenderness becomes a placid looking-glass in which each beholds the other; the mercurial wildness which no longer moves them is fixed behind this transparent screen, lending brightness to the mirrored images.

At any moment they may awake; Virginio will put on his pearl-coloured greatcoat and wrap an ermine tippet about Rosalba's throat, and the season being winter and very clear and cold, they will hurry to a fashionable pastry cook's to eat whipped cream and wafers.

THE END